Cut Up on Copacabana

David Scott

CUT UP ON COPACABANA

AND OTHER STORIES

DALKEY ARCHIVE PRESS

Copyright © 2018 by David Scott
First Dalkey Archive edition, 2018.

Library of Congress Cataloging-in-Publication Data
Identifiers: ISBN 978-1-62897-255-9
LC record available at https://catalog.loc.gov/

www.dalkeyarchive.com
Victoria, TX / McLean, IL / Dublin

Dalkey Archive Press publications are, in part, made possible through
the support of the University of Houston-Victoria and its programs in
creative writing, publishing, and translation.

Printed on permanent/durable acid-free paper

Contents

Schoolboy Rites of Passage

For Robin Fuller, Tom Lee, and Kevin Breathnach

I   Travel Notes

1. Cut Up on Copacabana

i   – Is that you when you were young?

– Yes that is me when I was *younger*. On holiday down on the farm.

– A pity about the spots – or were they freckles?

– Freckles, if you don't mind!

– And what are those plasters all over your chest?

– Oh, a slight accident.

– What'd you do, fall off a tractor?

– Nearly as bad. We were building a haystack and, at the tea-break, someone pitched their fork up into the bales. After tea, I was supposed to climb back up onto the stack to receive the bales passed up from the trailer. I took a flying leap up the side of the stack and caught my shoulder on the prongs of the fork.

– Golly!

– You never saw such a bloody mess: ripped right through my shirt and everything. I ended up with quite a few stitches.

– Poor Dad!

ii   – Can I come in?

– If you must.

– Hello!

– What do you want?

– Just wondering who was in here.

– You knew bloody well.

– You look different in the bath.

– Probably something to do with having wet hair.

– And what are those funny marks on your chest?

– Oh they are to remind me to turn the bath taps off –
when the water reaches a certain level; you know, a kind of
water mark.

– Very funny. Seriously, though, it looks as though you
were knifed.

– Nothing so exciting! No, it was a few years ago when
you were very small, just after we had the door into the garden
glazed. One evening, we were having a barbecue and I was
dashing back into the house to get some more drinks and I
smashed right through the glass door. One hell of a mess!

– Pity about the door.

– Never mind the bloody door!

iii   – You're turning a wonderful colour!

– Am I? Perhaps it's time I heaved over.

–   It must be the salt from the sea. I notice you didn't
bother to towel yourself after the last dip.

– No, it's much more fun to let the water evaporate in the
heat.

– Would you like me to rub in some suntan lotion?

– Yes, thank you.

– Hm, what are these elegant little scars across the top of
your chest?

– Oh yeah, really neat aren't they? I got them last autumn.

– What did you do, walk through a plate-glass window?

– No. It was during the cross-country season. We were
out in the sticks on a really boggy five-kilometre course, across
hedges and ditches and everything. I took a flying leap over a
bank but slipped in the mud and ended up impaling myself on
a bit of barbed wire fence. Unluckily for me, my body twisted
as I fell and so I ripped the flesh in three places.

– Christ!

– Yeah. And I was wearing spikes, which tells you how
slimy the ground was.

iv   – God, it's hot in here again today!

– Yeah, looks like it's going to be *torse nu* again.

– We'd better dump our gear in the corner of the court.

– You can tell me after the match about how you got those interesting-looking cuts on your shoulder.

– Nothing much to tell, actually. It happened when I was in Thailand last summer.

– Was that the swimming and canoeing trip you said you went on to see those islands off Thailand that were still unspoiled?

– Yeah.

– What did you do, get hooked by someone else's line?

– Very funny. No, I was snorkeling among the rocks and made a lunge for what looked like a fragment of coral or shell and scraped half my pec off against a submerged rock. It wasn't till I got out of the water that I realised what damage I'd done!

– Well, it doesn't look too bad now.

– So, now you can tell me your story about the meat cleaver when you were in New York.

– That's for later, after the game and over a pint!

v   – Just take off your shoes and your shirt and lie on the couch, please.

– What about my T-shirt?

– Oh, take that off too. That's it. Now, take a deep breath and hold it for a second. Okay, breathe out now. That's fine. All right.

– Can I get up now?

– Yes. Oh, just a minute. What are these scars?

– Don't you remember? A year or so back I developed a couple of – what are they called? – basal carcinomas.

– Oh yes. I sent you to Mr Keane. Well, he seems to have done a neat job.

– Yes. Quite a dab hand with a knife is Mr Keane. And

I was wide awake. All done under local anaesthetic. But the stitches looked really gruesome when they were fresh.

— But no recurrences since?

— Not so far, touch wood.

–And it didn't interfere with your trip to Brazil?

— Nope. Even went swimming in the Amazon.

vi   — Gee mate, how'd you cop those?

— What? Can I borrow some shampoo?

— Sure. Here. Those cuts.

— Oh, that happened last winter when I was in Brazil. I was jogging in the early evening along the beach at Copacabana when these two guys run up and pull a knife. I couldn't believe it. They were asking for dough, and there I was with nothing on but a pair of shorts.

— Real desperadoes by the sound of it.

— You're telling me! Gosh, this stuff is really soapy. Can you reach me my towel please? The blue one.

— Here you are.

— Thanks.

— So then what happened?

— One of them started pricking me with the tip of his knife blade. I didn't know what they expected me to do. I offered them my watch, but it was only a cheap chronometer I wear when I'm running. They weren't interested. So I pretended to fumble in my shorts pocket and then just made a dash for it. One of the sods threw his knife at me and it caught my left shoulder. But I just kept running.

— You're kidding.

— The hell I am! I was lucky to get away with just a few stitches.

— Did they ever catch the guys?

— I doubt it. Happens all the time in Rio.

2. Thirty-Six Ways of Looking at Mount Fuji

Umezawa in Sagami Province

Cranes fly into the dawn,
White mists swathe Fuji's peak
As indigo shadows recede from green pine forests.

In the mountains of Totomi Province

Framed by triangles of timber supporting a giant log,
Distant Fuji soars;
Woodcutters saw as the black smoke of a charcoal fire
Mimics the white clouds writhing about the mountain.

Mistuma Pass in the Province of Kai

The noble angle of Fuji's distant flank
Is bisected by a giant pine tree;
Travellers stretch arms to measure its girth
As clouds billow atop and about the mountain's peak.

Great Wave off Kanagawa

A giant wave is about to break
Over buffeted manned canoes,
But the rearing surf is ignored
By the distant beacon of snow-capped Fuji.

The Island of Tsukuda

Ships' masts prick the sky
Above the wooded island settlement,
While distant Fuji's white knife blade
Slices through the pine-forested horizon.

Ushibori in the Province of Hitachi

A barge is beached in the rushes of Kasumi-ga-ura;
Two snowy herons, disturbed by rice-water poured overboard,
Take flight
As Fuji's white profile rises against the approaching darkness.

Kajakazawa in the Province of Kai

A fisherman casts diagonal lines
Into the blue torrent of Fuji river;
The mountain's cone emerges from mist
Into a band of amber sunlight.

Eijiri in the Province of Suruga

Travellers bend double in the face of a stiff breeze;
Leaves, hats and paper scatter across the reedy flats;
The distant Fuji pulls at its guy ropes like a kite barely tethered.

Minobu River

Minobu River rolls like watered silk down the valley;
Along its undulating course, travellers mount and descend;
Fuji's cone peaks between distant Chinese mountains,
Swathed in cloud.

Surugadai in Edo

Figures mount and descend the path by the blue Kanda river;
Trees and foliage shimmer in the azure heat;
Only distant Fuji stays cool beneath its melting ice cap.

Hodogaya on the Tokaido

A frieze of picturesque travellers passes in the foreground;
A screen of pines gesticulates against an azure sky;
Far beyond, Mount Fuji bares its indigo southern slopes
to the spring sunlight.

Honjo Tatekawa, Edo

Across stacked beams and planks in a waterside timber yard,
Pairs of rods rest like giant chopsticks;
Dwarfing the riverside houses opposite,
Palisades of poles obscure the distant Fuji.

Senju in the Province of Musashi

A packhorse chafes the ground by the floodgate over the Senju
River;
Fishermen cast their rods
As the muleteer gazes across the paddy field to Mount Fuji.

Sekiya-n-Sato on the Sumida River

Three Samurai gallop their horses along the winding causeway
above the flooded paddy fields;

A pine tree leans precariously over the Musashino plain;
The colour of bark, the lower slopes of Mount Fuji rise, red-
brown, above the distant plantations.

Red Fuji

Mount Fuji rears its gigantic red-brown cone into the blue of
high summer;
Stratocumulus clouds mottle the sky
While dark green pine forests stubble the mountain's massive
base.

Ono Shinden in the Province of Suruga

Oxen laden with reeds pass along a country road;
Five herons fly in diagonal formation across the misty fenland;
Far beyond, Mount Fuji rises imperceptibly from the watery
plain, its flanks widening beneath bands of vapour.

The Gay Quarters at Serigu

A *daimyo*'s procession marches across the foreground;
The last musket-bearer shades his eyes to look across the rice
fields, where two women sit watching the soldiers, towards the
distant Fuji;
Fingers of water and, higher up, cloud, encroach upon the scene
but spare the neat angularity of the Gay Quarters.

Tea Garden at Katakura in Suruga Province

Under an azure sky, tea is being picked, dried, baled and transported by woman, man and animal;
A blue stream meanders through the plantation;
White fingers of cloud move from the north towards Mount Fuji's snowy flank.

The Bay at Tago

Fishing boats' long prows cut through the blue surge;
Figures on the distant grey shore rake and store salt in mat-covered shacks;
Far beyond Mount Fuji rises like a sapphire wave above the ochre mist that swathes its wooded lower slopes.

Kanaya on the Tokaido

Near naked porters wade to and fro across the ford between Kanaya and Shimada;
In the folds of stylized sapphire waves, bales of goods and palanquins are carried by teams, while single porters shoulder individual travellers;
In the distance, Mount Fuji rises, seemingly indifferent to the scene.

Enoshima in the Province of Sagami

At low tide, travellers from Kawakura venture across the sandbank to Sagami Island;
A pagoda rises above wooded gardens behind the village;

In the bay, the mast and rigging of a solitary moored craft point
to Mount Fuji, far beyond.

Nakahara in the province of Sagami

A motley crew of travellers passes to and fro along and across a
shallow stream;
A fisherman is intent on his net, a peasant woman on balancing
child, hoe, kettle and food tray, a peddler on the pole carrying
his boxes of wares;
Only one figure turns to look at the taught diagonal line of
Mount Fuji's distant flank.

Sunset over Ryogoku Bridge seen from Oumaya Pier

The laden ferry's curved keel rocks on the undulating swell;
The distant Ryogoku Bridge spans upwards in a reverse ellipse;
The city's profile on the far bank darkens as evening turns Fuji's
cone to ink;
The whole scene – a harmony in black, indigo and green.

Lake Suwa in the Province of Shinano

The sky at sunset is washed with bands of indigo, azure and
amber;
A lone vessel returns across the pearlescent lake;
A solitary shrine in the foreground rises from the blue shadows
beside two ancient pines;
Its conical roof echoes the distant beacon of Mount Fuji.

Shichirigahama in the Province of Sagami

Waves break against the shore;
The coast rises, luring the eye to a blue, wooded isthmus
That in turn leads to a view of Mount Fuji
Rising from mists into a honey-coloured haze
Topped by the azure and indigo of the heavens.

Tamagawa River in the Province of Musashi

A blue tree silhouetted against emerald vegetation reaches
towards the river where a horse drinks;
A ferryman crosses to the far bank, the prow of his craft pointing
towards the distant Fuji
Whose indigo lower slopes rise above green forests and a beer-co-
loured mist that swathes the farther shore.

The Hongan-ji Temple at Asakusa in Edo

In the right foreground, roofers repair the massive ornamental
gable of the temple;
To the left, a flimsy scaffold and a kite rise above the mists that
flow like custard over the city rooves –
From which emerges Mount Fuji, like a sugar-loaf.

Snowy Morning in Koishikawa

A drinking party on the veranda of a summer house surveys the
snowy cityscape;
A woman points to three birds cavorting high above the
snow-laden pines and roof gables;

In the distance, Mount Fuji rises like an iced loaf on a white
table.

Fujimihara in the Province of Owari

A cooper works within the hoop of a gigantic tub;
Circles of green bamboo and tools of the trade litter the ground;
Through the wooden ring, beyond the pearly rice-paddies, a
distant Fuji rises above the wooded horizon.

The Miksui Store at Suruga-machi in Edo

The street descends between gabled shops selling dry goods;
A roofer flings a bundle up to another on the steep-pitched roof;
Kites soar high into the breeze that has cleared the air around
the distant snow-capped Fuji.

The Bay at Noboto

Fisher-folk collect shellfish from the jade-coloured shallows
beneath the gateways to the shrine;
Further out, fishing boats zigzag towards the far shore;
Mount Fuji rises white and distant, framed within an angle of
the sacred gate.

The 'Round Cushion' Pine at Aoyama

Edo citizens, drinking saké, survey the scene;
A pine green dome of shade obliterates all beneath except the leg
of a gardener sweeping pine needles;
The distant Fuji rises grey and severe above bands of silver cloud.

Thunderstom below the Mountain

The colour of rusting iron, Fuji's massive cone rises;
Forks of lightning zigzag against its darkened lower slopes;
Blue skies shine down on cumulus clouds and pine forests.

Dawn at Isawa in the Province of Kai

A blue-green knoll rises like a wave above the main street in
Isawa;
A procession of travellers moves out, the chill dawn reflected in
their white hats;
Mount Fuji rises, bottle-green above the bands of silvery mist.

Climbing the Mountain

Pilgrims carrying staffs and a ladder clamber up the tortuous
mountain paths;
Clouds swirl in the deep valleys scarring the volcanic slopes;
Higher up, travellers crouch in a cave, huddled together against
the cold.

The Waterwheel at Onden

The waterwheel disgorges its measured cascades into the mill-
stream;
Peasants shoulder sacks of grain and water barrels;
A boy leads his pet tortoise on a string, diagonally opposite the
distant Mount Fuji.

3. Enjoying the Scenery

In 1962, the holiday of my grandmother's choice was a Leroy Tour advertised as 'Gems of Italy with Paris and the Riviera'. As a fourteen-year-old boy, I was to accompany her on this Easter trip, which for years after was referred to as 'our holiday', a record of which I kept in a diary written in a school exercise book. The Leroy blurb included the usual travel-brochure hyperbole that I was happy to transpose to my account, in which were experienced 'breath-taking' or 'scenic' views as we sped along 'auto-strada', 'gastronomic' delights, and numerous visits to 'basilicas' and other memorable sights. My preparations for the trip included buying a suitcase off the back of a cornflakes box, packing my school cadet-force khaki shirt and shorts (I was sure it would be hot) and trying to find two weeks' supply of matching socks.

The first stage of the trip involved a night at the Grosvenor Hotel in London in which I was allocated an enormous double room. I felt I had to do justice to the space by sleeping alternately in the two giant beds and using as often as possible the vast en suite bathroom. The next day, the travel party assembled at the Victoria Coach Station for the afternoon ride along the recently completed M2 motorway to the cross-Channel airport at Lydd. The party included: Mary and Katie, two spinster sisters from Newcastle; a very loud woman, her mother and female friend – I remember hearing the first of this trio announcing 'I know every inch of Monaco'; a married couple from the North with a pronounced Yorkshire accent; a dutiful bachelor son with well-Brylcreemed hair, escorting an aging mother and maiden aunt; three girls, all very pretty, from Norwich, London and Canada respectively; a fat lady; a pair of pensioners from Australia; and a rather sharp young couple.

While awaiting the Silver City flight – delayed, as Katie wryly commented, by 'unfavorable atmospheric conditions' – in a Bristol Freighter aircraft, members of the group 'palled up' with each other, my grandmother being befriended by the Newcastle spinsters Mary and Katie with whom we consorted for the rest of the trip. Guessing and other games were played to while away the time. 'I am a famous French sportsman, husband to Edith Piaf,' the Fat Lady directed at me. As my mind went momentarily blank, she replied, unnecessarily loudly I thought, 'Marcel Cerdan, the boxer: I thought you'd have known that!' As a boxing enthusiast, I was doubly humiliated by this publicly advertised failure, even though Cerdan was of a generation before the boxers such as Floyd Patterson in whom I was interested.

The wardrobes of the ladies scarcely changed over the following two weeks, regardless of temperature or time of day. Mary wore a drab-coloured linen jacket, skirt and sensible shoes. Katie was enveloped in a long grey gaberdine coat resembling a dressing gown, set off by a woolly bonnet; this get-up made her look as though she were sleepwalking: all she needed to complete the effect was a candle and snuffer. My grandmother wore a purple wool suit enlivened by embroidered satin 'fronts' that were pinned across her bosom to her copious underwear. All I remember of the girls' dresses is that they were always pretty and that in Italy they did not wear their nylon stockings. The men wore sports jackets and open-neck shirts. I wore a variation on my school uniform: white or grey shirt, grey flannels, school tie, but no cap or blazer; a crew-neck sweater was a concession to casualness but was soon relinquished in Italy where my CCF khakis became the order of the day.

On arrival in Le Touquet, the party was ushered by our courier, Paul Bentley, a handsome Maltese (suffering as it later emerged form stress-induced ulcers), to the waiting Berliet Randonnée coach, piloted by a silent French driver called Emile. The smell of new plastic was one of the initial charms of the voyage as was the possibility of observing the foreign makes of car that sped along the French roads. I was always favoured with a window seat as my grandmother, next to whom I sat for most of the trip, preferred to, as she said, 'get her leg out' into the corridor running between the seats. It was agreed that couples would on a daily basis move a seat backwards (those at the very back returning to the front) to afford as far as possible equal comfort and convenience to all. I, however, got a couple of extra goes in the back seat with the pretty girls as some of the more elderly passengers were willing to forgo this pleasure.

The only notable incident of the first leg of the trip was the enquiry addressed to my grandmother in a loud Bradford twang: 'Is your grandson enjoying the scenery?' – delivered by one of the Yorkshire couple, two rows ahead of us in the coach, whom I had just observed opening their window to deposit rubbish into the passing landscape. There was a tea-break halfway between Le Touquet and Paris at a café where I stepped for a first time into a world of language, gestures and smells that were authentically French: boys were larking and swearing in the street, while the smell of fresh coffee and Gauloises pervaded the air. The arrival in Paris was in its turn authenticated by a first glimpse of the Eiffel Tower, though I was surprised to discover it was painted brown and not black as I had always imagined. The first night was spent in the Hôtel du Nord in Paris where, after a late supper of steak and salade à la française, the tired party repaired to bed. My room near the top of the hotel was decorated in dirty red chintz; the wiring was faulty – the bedside lights kept flashing on and off – but I was impressed by the bidet, the first I had seen, into which I took a perverse delight in pissing.

The itinerary of Day Two was a drive from Paris to Lyon

via Auxerre and Avallon, with a midday break for lunch. The Burgundy landscape flashed past with few points of recognition and without incident except that soon after the departure from Avallon one of the girls discovered she'd left her bag at the restaurant. A heated discussion ensued as to whether the coach should return to recover the missing purse of the distraught young lady but it was eventually decided that at the next stop the courier would telephone back and request the mislaid item be forwarded to the hotel in Rome, a couple of days ahead. After this little drama, the girl dried her tears and the company relapsed into a state of soporific well-being until the coach arrived at Lyon.

The third day of the Tour marked a shift into the exotic: bright sun, long straight roads with light filtered by plane trees flickering across the path of the coach, new scents and flavours. A stop-off at Montélimar to eat *nougat* (never again to be pronounced 'nuggate'), to buy sunglasses (black plastic with rectangular lenses), to take off the school tie and jumper and try to appear more like a white-shirted Mediterranean male than an English schoolboy. Monuments and scenery in the bright light suddenly began to take on a photogenic quality, so the ancient box camera, borrowed from a sister, came out of its canvas bag and was used to photograph the Roman arch at Orange and the old ladies in front of a fountain at Avignon. Meanwhile, I was aware that the girls, all in their summer dresses, were chatting and laughing over ice creams at an adjacent café. As we got underway again, the Mediterranean coast came into view, the balmy air and swaying palms completing an idyllic picture of the Côte d'Azur.

Day Four took the coach party from Nice to Viareggio in a drive along the French and Italian Mediterranean coast. First stop Monaco, (every inch of which, I remembered, was known by the Loud Woman member of the party), where the courier Paul regaled his captive audience with the romantic wedding of

Prince Rainier and Princess Grace, the fortunes won and lost in the Casinos, the high life of southern France. The passage into Italy was seamless beneath a blue sky and the journey along the modern Italian roads as uneventful as it was exhilarating. A minor crisis was faced, however, at the Hotel in Viareggio were some passengers were obliged to share rooms. I found myself teamed up with the dutiful son in the Mother and maiden aunt party. 'I was so relieved to hear I would be sharing a room with you' he kindly said, urging me later to use his hair cream if I liked. The business of who used the bathroom first, of who rose when, and of dressing and undressing in the same room, was tactfully managed. I decided it would be more manly to sleep in my pajama bottoms only and in the morning I turned up for breakfast in a clean white shirt with my hair styled in a quiff using the borrowed Brylcreem.

From Viareggio there was a day trip to Pisa and Florence. This was the first day on which I sat in the back seat of the bus with the three girls, their summer dresses, fragrance, and the warmth of the day contriving to give me an erection that stayed with me the length of the first leg of the trip. On arrival at Pisa, leaving my grandmother and her spinster friends to explore the Cathedral and Baptistery, I decided to climb the leaning tower: the breeze that circulated around it and entered my shirt cooled me somewhat, but the exertion of the climb and slight vertigo that accompanied arrival at the top, and the contemplation of the oblique view afforded of the city of Pisa, led to a resurgence of the sexual urge: realising I was alone at the top of the leaning tower, I unbuttoned my trousers, disentangled my tumescent cock from my underpants, and began to rub it against the marble of the inner wall of the arcade. At the point of ejaculation, I heard footsteps mounting the tower and had just the time to wipe myself off with my handkerchief before retreating down the stairs past the approaching tourists, an elderly couple sweating profusely on their climb. The coach party were already assembling for departure when I rushed up, flushed and exhilarated. 'What kept you so long up the tower?' my grandmother innocently enquired, to which without thinking I replied: 'Oh, I was just enjoying the scenery'. I spent the rest of the journey to Florence in an agony of embarrassment in case the girls on the back seat beside me should smell the fresh sperm that still besmeared the handkerchief that I had stuffed back into my trouser pocket.

The visit to Florence in the heat of the afternoon, with its rugged masculine palaces juxtaposed with feminine churches and baptistery, its naked statues set among clumps of fragrant flowers, rekindled the morning's arousal. I spent much time staring at the sculpture in the Loggia della Signoria, in particular Perseus and the Medusa, and Michelangelo's David. I contemplated the perfect musculature of Perseus with envy, rolling down my shirtsleeves in shame as I compared my skinny arms to his bronze biceps. But it was the gigantic beauty of my homonym David that affected me most, and in particular the loosely hanging hands that seemed, though very fine, to me overlarge for the body – hands that had been used to select and then sling a stone to slay Goliath. I thought with shame of my own hands that had been put to a somewhat different purpose that morning in Pisa. The dive into the cool of the Uffizi Gallery later in the afternoon came as a relief, as the calming presence of the Raphael madonnas, much admired by the girls and the spinster ladies, tempered the heat of my earlier experiences. The purchase of postcards and colour slides was an additional distraction, in particular the challenge of sending postcard messages using only five words and so qualifying for a cheaper postal rate. So later that evening I scrawled on all my cards: 'Enjoying the scenery – love – David'.

The climax of the tour was the three days spent in Rome, 'the Eternal City'. The hotel, located not far from the wedding-cake Victor Emmanuel Monument, was spacious, marble and cool. I once again had a room to myself, but was at a loss as to what to do about the accumulating pile of sweaty socks and shirts with grubby collars. I tried soaking the former in the bidet and decided from then on to stick to wearing the CCF khakis which at least did not show the dirt. (This was a time before the advent of cheap T-shirts and boxer shorts.) Nevertheless, the days in Rome were memorable, not least in that they brought to three-dimensional reality the black-and-white photos that enlivened my school Latin textbooks. The Roman Forum was exactly as illustrated, with its broken columns and the Arch of Constantine. There was the circular Temple of Vesta that had always fascinated – though its significance eluded me, and there the Colosseum: here as my Latin master had told us, were staged boxing matches with fighters using the brutal, lead-weighted *caestus*, tussles with wild beasts (the story of Androcoles and the Lion was vivid in my memory) and chariot races. The Fontana di Trevi was by comparison a tawdry, effeminate affair, its tarnished accumulation of *lire* coins only just being compensated by the fountain's association with the astonishing image of the blond Anita Eckberg rising in her black ball gown from the waters as filmed in Frederico Fellini's recently released movie *La Dolce Vita*.

The image of the full-bosomed goddess was doubtless not high in the consciousness of my grandmother's spinster friend Mary, who nevertheless accompanied me on many memorable visits to baroque Italian churches, whose names – San Giovanni in Laterano, Santa Maria Maggiore – rolled off the tongue as delectably as the waters of the Trevi fountain flowed off Eckberg's magnificent shoulders. Her head swathed in a lacy scarf, Mary led me round the cavernous interior of St Peter's church, most of the famous sculptures (including Michelangelo's *Piétà*) regrettably being covered as it was just before Easter. Once again, the riddle of a Roman image in my Latin textbook was solved: the great circular space in front of the basilica was carved out by broad embracing arms of Bernini's colonnades. Another surprise was the vacant clerestory hole in the domed ceiling of the Roman Pantheon. An afternoon trip to more ancient Roman remains at the old port of Ostia, another to the catacombs that run beneath part of the city, were topped by a visit to the athletic stadium constructed for the Rome Olympics of 1960: once again I was awe-inspired by the elegance and imagined prowess of the athletes and boxers whose white marble statues surround the track.

Back at the front of the bus with my grandmother, the next stage of the trip took us from Rome to Pesaro on the Adriatic coast via Perugia and Assisi. A visit to the vaults of the church in Assisi was memorable: I had never seen so many or such large white candles, the smell of candlewick and incense contriving again to stimulate movements in my body that were the opposite of religious. The late afternoon light as we sped on our way through the Apennines towards the Adriatic coast was mellow and golden, enhancing the appearance of the grey-blue waters of the approaching sea. By contrast, the hotel in Pesaro where we stayed was cheap and tawdry: the place smelt of plumbing, the furnishings were drab and the bread rolls at supper were stale. Letters of complaint to the travel agency were already being drafted by certain members of the party as the tireless courier Paul tried to put things to right with the management.

The highlight of Pesaro for me was being taken by the Loud Lady, her mother and friend 'out on the town': sprucing myself up as best I could with my school tie and blazer, I accompanied the ladies to a bar near the hotel where they proceeded to regale me with accounts of their social life at home. 'Lucky at cards, unlucky in love'. 'Easy come, easy go'. The Loud Lady explained how she would go out wearing her fur coat but on arrival at the party would 'slip it off' and replace it by a fur stole – an account accompanied by appropriate hand gestures and movement of the shoulders. The other two ladies allowed this performance to go on without murmur, sipping their gin and orange with equanimity as, cool as a cucumber, I drank my beer. Trying to create the impression that this kind of conversation was the most normal thing in the world, I escorted the tipsy group safely back to the hotel where they assembled for a nightcap with the rest of the party at the hotel bar. Here, I was duly complimented by the ladies on my gentlemanly conduct throughout the evening, an accolade that earned me a conspiratorial wink from the courier Paul and a smirk from the girls.

The next leg of the trip was the most romantic as we drove through the Italian countryside to Verona, the city of Romeo and Juliet. Here we visited Juliet's house with its picturesque stone balcony, and the fine Roman amphitheatre. The romance of the situation was somewhat marred, however, on arrival at the hotel in front of which the coach parked rather awkwardly. In the end the backseat passengers (myself and the three girls) were obliged to get out via the emergency exit, causing me to embarrass the last girl out (she from Norwich) by shouting at her to shut the door before the bus moved off. I disgraced myself further the same evening when, at dinner in the hotel restaurant, conversation at our table (that of my Grandmother, Mary and Katie) turned towards the qualities of the dutiful son sitting at the adjacent table with his mother and aunt. At that very moment the son happened to smile in our direction so I foolishly blurted out to him, to the embarrassment of all, 'Your ears must be burning!' Fortunately the well-meaning gaucheness of the fourteen-year-old boy was laughed off at both tables.

From Verona, we took a day trip to Venice, a city the 'sights' of which were already familiar to me through the deckle-edged postcards my mother had sent from there the summer before after an Italian holiday. So gondolas on blue canals, the pink and white Doge's Palace, St Mark's Square and the Bridge of Sighs were all clichés that after experience in reality were filed away again in my postcard-collection memory. However, some perceptions, outmanœuvering the realm of déjà vu, succeeded in conjuring up some of the magic of the place: rounding a corner into an expected square to find that it was a canal; looking across at churches that were in fact divided from the viewer by a stretch of water; wandering streets where there was no motor traffic and in which the rhythm of walking was correspondingly adjusted. For many of the members of the party, my grandmother included, Venice meant glass, so there were expeditions to shops and showrooms and even a glass-blowing factory. My grandmother bought as a souvenir for my mother six brandy bubbles, each inscribed 'N' for Napoleon in gold, and each a different colour – Venetian colours: ruby, turquoise, sapphire, zircon, emerald and topaz. I thought they were the most beautiful glasses I had ever seen. Meanwhile, not to be outdone, other members of the party set off in pursuit of multi-coloured glass beads that the couple from Yorkshire had spied in a small shop down a side alley. I thought that the whole party returned that evening to Verona with Venetian light reflected in their eyes.

Day Twelve marked a shift into a different scenic gear as the 'Gems of Italy' were forsaken for the excitement of an Alpine drive that took the party via the Italian lakes across the St Gotthard Pass to Lake Luçerne. The clearness of the air, the vividness of the blues and greens, the shimmering of the lakes, was an unexpected delight. The hotel in Brunnen was situated by the water. I remember on arriving in my room leaning out of the window to view the lake and encountering the smile of the courier Paul who, lodged in an adjacent room, was similarly basking in his shirtsleeves at his open window taking in the Alpine panorama. It was at that moment that I felt I was in the process of becoming a sophisticated European traveller, a role that the charming, urbane and multilingual Paul played to perfection. Another pleasure of the hotel was the feather-down quilt, the first I had experienced (this being a decade before duvets became standard in Britain). That evening, there was a Romantic trip on the lake in a candle-lit boat. I dutifully escorted the old ladies of my party though was constantly drawn by the giggles of the girls coming from another part of the boat. The ladies talked of previous trips to Switzerland (Interlaken, Montreux) and my grandmother regaled the Newcastle spinsters with accounts of the outrageous behaviour of a sister-in-law, my great aunt Jane, who at Lausanne had scolded her niece for 'dancing with a nigger'.

It was in Switzerland, towards the end of the itinerary, that I felt the charm of the trip most intensely: waking up each morning in a different hotel room, anticipating the new sights and scenery that the day would bring. As we set off from Brunnen I remember deeply envying a young Swiss cyclist who went whirring downhill past the coach on his racing bike, wishing I could change identity with him and myself become a dynamic part of the extraordinary surrounding scene.

The final two days' itinerary passed into a blur of places and names as the coach took the party through lowland Switzerland, France, Luxemburg and Belgium. I have no memory of Brussels except for a dark and Gothic-looking hotel where the party were split into two, one section being housed in an adjacent annex. Unfortunately the young women were housed in a different part of the hotel from me and, determined to enjoy their final night on the continent, went off gaily to explore the bars of the city. Marooned in our quarters after dinner, my grandmother and I were invited by the stalwart Mary and Katie to join them in their room for a nightcap: travelling Primus, kettle and tea were produced, and it was in this melancholy fashion that my last night of the trip was celebrated

The last day of the trip was mostly taken up by the monotonous drive along the northern plains of Belgium and France, past numerous First World War memorials and graveyards. The last few kilometers of the trip were marred by the embarrassment of the question of the tip for Paul, the courier, who felt he had been inadequately rewarded for his pains, and then, on arrival back in England, by a little drama at the customs at Lydd. Mrs Fur Coat, attempting to bring into the country a camera she had bought in Switzerland without paying import duty, had asked the Canadian girl, as a Commonwealth visitor, to carry it for her. The ploy was unfortunately foiled, leaving the hapless Paul, already out of pocket, to lend her the money to pay the fine since Mrs Fur Coat did not have sufficient cash on her.

The farewells at Victoria Coach Station were unexpectedly poignant. I was particularly moved by the pleasant compliments – 'a fine young man', 'will be a credit to his family' – and genuine good wishes bestowed on me by members of the party (such as the Australian couple and the Fat Lady) who had seemed less sympathetic during the trip. The return journey to Norwich from London by train was enlivened by the unexpected company of one of the three girls on the tour, the one whom I had inadvertently shouted at in Verona. It emerged that she had been Paul's consort throughout the trip and that he had related to her his health problems, in particular the ulcers that the stress of his job seemed to have inflicted upon him. My grandmother was all agog.

The diary of 'Our Holiday' that I had scrawled in the school exercise book, was written up properly in a larger ledger incorporating the many postcards and photos I had amassed during the trip. My chief souvenir, the black sunglasses were to my chagrin soon lost. There was correspondence for several subsequent Christmases with Mary and Katie, who sent cards that my grandmother referred to as of the 'Holy Ghost' variety. On the first Christmas after the trip I received from Paul a pleasant message with a photograph of himself standing in his shirtsleeves smiling in the sun, enjoying the scenery, on a hill overlooking Florence.

4. Dynamo Dave

It was one of those blindingly bright Australian afternoons: the waters of Sydney Harbour were glittering against the opposite shore while the porcelain spinnakers of the opera house glistened and the girders of the harbour bridge groaned in the heat. I was lounging about in Circular Quay waiting for the ferry that would take me home across the water to Manly. My attention was caught by a lanky figure lolling at the waterside, listening intently to the aboriginal musicians playing on the esplanade. A cross between Crocodile Dundee and an off-duty World War II soldier, the tall frame was clothed in varying shades of khaki – shirt, shorts, acubra – that reflected the colour of his eyes, skin, and what was visible of his hair. There seemed to be a faintly exotic tinge to this ochre harmony that set the man apart and drew me to him. He was smoking a cigarette, which was sufficient excuse to approach him for a light.

– Hey mate, could I bother you for a spark?
– Sure, here you are.
– You're not from these parts, I guess.
– How can you tell, he replied with a smile.
– I dunno. Just an intuition. Where *are* you from?
– Dynamo Island.
– Where?
– Dynamo Island,
– Where's that?
– It's in the middle of the North Atlantic Ocean between Europe and America.
– How come I've never heard of it?
– It's small – by Australian standards, and to you it's the antipodes.

– And so what brings you to Aus?

– I read a book that said it was once the world's biggest and best-kept estate.

– Oh yeah, I read that book too. It speaks to quite a lot of us in Australia. Does it connect in any way to your island?

– Yes, to the extent that it's about an attempt to maintain harmony between man, the animal and vegetable world and the natural environment.

– So people like to get out and about in Dynamo, you're a nature-loving folk?

– In Dynamo people don't feel they're separate from nature; they're part of it. Everything connects with everything else. This is one of the lessons the indigenous people of Australia also seem to have cottoned on to. So in Dynamo everywhere and everything is out and about.

– Yeah, but you do have cities too, I guess.

– We do, and the coastal ones are a bit like Sydney. There is the same separation between nature and city, but one in which both are in contact with each other. Dynamo's capital is like a Sydney with no cars: apart from trams and trains (which are public), everyone's on a bike, in a boat, or on their feet – even on an animal – we still use horses a lot in Dynamo.

– I guess then most Dynamoans are lean and mean like yourself as they have to get around under their own steam.

– You're dead right. For Dynamoans the human body is to nature what the mind is to the city. The town must look after the country as it pumps life into it; ditto, the mind's getting the larger picture means it also gets the underlying nature of the world. To neglect the body is seen as a kind of lunacy. So the whole of nature is a gym and people try to blend in.

– Is that why you're dressed in khaki – so you can disappear into the landscape? Or is there also a military connection?

– Ha ha, yeah, maybe so. Nobody wants to be a blot on the landscape, especially one that's green and lush like Dynamo.

As for the military, all Dynamoans do a year's social or military service, so that they can learn what's at stake in social life: the unavoidability of violence (defending the city) as well as the need for caring.

– So Dynamoans think war is inevitable, like the neo-cons?

– No, they don't think that it's inevitable – certainly not in 2015 with so much to learn from the disasters of the twentieth century. The Dynamoan military is largely defensive; its aim is to protect the country's freedom and independence. It's a bit like boxing: you learn how to fight and show your mettle in the ring, but you never challenge another man (or woman) outside of it. The aim is to have the capability of violence but never to use it except in extreme defensive situations.

– Talking of which, what about sports, are they as popular in Dynamo as here in Aus?

– Every bit, especially those that still connect with the natural world like swimming, sailing, running, hunting; but also team sports for their social value (rugby, cricket) and boxing – the Dynamoans are particularly keen on this sport – and not just as a deterrent as I just suggested.

– Why's that?

– Because boxing teaches a hell of a lot about human interaction with the physical and the way mental and physical inter-react. You look like a pretty fit guy yourself, what are you into?

– Running, and I have a building interest in boxing too, and am happy to chuck around any projectile – cricket or rugby ball, whatever comes to hand. I love the challenge of cross-country endurance runs: they teach you something like what you were saying the Dynamo lifestyle opens up. Here in Aus, though, we are only relearning what the right balance is – partly from indigenous people. It's always puzzled me that for athletes of the past, sporting ability was a gift rather than a practice. For my grandpa's generation training hard reduced the purity of your talent. For me training is the means and the ends.

– Yeah, I know what you mean. In Dynamo, training for sport is a kind of ritual, a hygiene that every one can practise. It's a like dance, a way of putting the body (and its urges) through the motions in a physically and socially enjoyable way.

– In Aus and elsewhere in the West, people tend to separate masculinized sports and other body arts from things like dance that are thought of as being more performative and feminine. One of the things I like about shadow boxing is that you only need to tweak it slightly and it becomes a dance. In a sense dance seems to be at the core of all sports.

– I agree, sports and dance are like ritual re-enactments of the human body's urges: the beauty of them is that they harmonize and socialize physical energy and desire.

They help keep things in balance.

– Yeah, keeping the balance right is the main thing. It's like food and drink. Talking of which, would you fancy a pint of something cooling?

– I never say no to that. Just quietly, we call 'em schooners here mate.

– And here's a brochure you can look over later: it'll tell you more about Dynamo:

Dynamo Island

Dynamo is an island the size of England situated in the North Atlantic Ocean on a similar latitude to France. Roughly circular in shape, it has high granitic (Cambrian) mountains along its western extremity (the Handlebar Mountains) with long limestone escarpments (the Freewheel Plains) stretching eastward. As the prevailing winds are westerly, the rainfall in the mountains is high, resulting in dense deciduous forest with many rushing streams. The easterly plains are drier and ideal for arable farming. The island's main river, the Crease, gathers many

eastward lowing tributaries before reaching its mouth in a long
estuary at Veloxeter, the country's capital and main port.

Lacking significant reserves of coal or oil, the country's
government from the beginning of the twentieth century
developed a policy of maximal energy conservation and intense
environmental protection. Over half of the country's electricity
is generated by waterpower, with about a third by tide- and
wind-power. A highly developed public transport system
based on electric trains and trams obviated the necessity for
cars. On short trips, city- and country-dwellers alike use bikes,
with many in the country travelling by pony and trap. Since
there are no tractors, carthorses continue to do the work of
ploughing and haulage. This has resulted in a slower rhythm of
work but one that has no negative environmental impact. An
intensive recycling system means that little is wasted and there
is a national ban on plastic (except for electronic, medical and
communicational goods). Pesticides and all artificial fertilizers
are also banned. All fowl and animals are free-range, the concept
of factory-farming being unknown.

This approach to agriculture and the environment means
that the country's internal economy is as much based on local
self-sufficiency and regional exchange as on the centralised,
supermarket culture of Europe and North America. Every house
in the country is encouraged to have its own garden and every
small town has its weekly market. Although predominantly
agrarian, the country is quite rich since its cheap and abundant
electrical power has enabled it to develop sophisticated electrical
and mechanical technology. It is a world leader in bicycle design.
Though lacking in coal and oil, the country has good reserves of
iron ore and, in the Handlebar Mountains, base metals.

A national computer and telecommunications network
promotes work at home and reduces the need for daily travel.
As a further saving in power, the country's towns and cities use
their streetlights only between sundown and 1 a.m., while in the
country – owing to the lack of pollution and light interference –

people are less dependent on artificial light. All bikes and pony traps are fitted with dynamos and all homes powered by solar panels. Wood fires are permitted but only if fuelled by faggots collected in the country's many oak and beech forests.

Cycling is the country's national sport, though cricket, rugby, boxing and rowing are extremely popular. All these sports are taught in the state schools, along with swimming, riding and tennis. There is an annual national cycling championship (the Dynamo Cup, equivalent to the Tour de France), open to women and men, as well as national rugby and cricket leagues. National service of one year is compulsory for all eighteen-year-olds, with both sexes entering the army, air force and naval services or serving apprenticeships in hospitals, schools and other national institutions. The naval tradition in the country is very strong, the chief naval centre being Hadrianopolis on the south coast.

Dynamo is a democratic republic, without monarch or aristocracy. There is no national religion, though faiths are tolerated provided they do not assert their differences in ostentatious communitarianism. An ancient mythology attached to agrarian, maritime and sporting accomplishments is popularly cultivated and reflected in many regional team mascots and badges. The national flag is a rectangle divided longwise, with the upper band (blue) representing the sky, the lower (green) the earth. In the centre figures a white wheel with eight spokes, the symbolic dynamo linking earth and sky and ensuring a cyclical replenishment of both spheres. The circle is a national symbol, promoted both as an aesthetic principle and as a model of community and of energy, mobility and productivity.

Self-deprecatory humour is a national characteristic and although individual success is admired and encouraged, much importance is attached to teamwork and communal effort. The western cult of celebrity is looked on with skepticism. Pleasure and self-fulfillment are encouraged in particular through outdoor activities, sports, games and entertainment. The country produces fine wines and beers, excellent fish, fruit and vegetables. All drugs and stimulants (including alcohol) are legalized, though those imported from abroad are expensive, and addiction is strongly discouraged. The island is conscious of its status as a cog in the larger global wheel but fully aware of its function and of the need to produce energy in a way that is not harmful to its environment, national or international.

It is not by accident therefore that cycling is the country's national sport. It is promoted not only as an enjoyable sport in its own right, as an excellent form of exercise for both sexes and all ages, and as a highly efficient means of transport, but also for *ethical* reasons: the bicycle enables humans to enter into a constructive relationship with the physical environment in which energy, movement and a sense of the real resistance and forces at play in the natural world and in the human body are recognized. The idea of producing power from human energy that is put to human use within a balanced ecological equation is central to Dynamo Island's understanding of man's role in the world. The dynamo principle thus became central to the island community's ethos and is reflected not only in the country's name but also in much of its national symbolism. The annual Tour of Dynamo cycle race that lasts for ten days and is open to men and women within a wide range of categories, constitutes a kind of national celebration of this principle. In taking its participants on a spectacular route through all the eight provinces of the country (including Maurice Island) it also draws public attention to the beauty and variety of the island's natural scenery.

5. Airborne Alipio

I'm sitting in the American Airways Boeing, an empty seat between me and the window, through which I'm studying the new livery of United Airlines on a neighbouring aircraft. Just before take-off, the vacant place is occupied by a tall and apparently hairless young black wearing off-white chinos and a navy blue T-shirt whose sleeves are rolled to reveal perfect biceps. I watch fascinated through the first hour of the flight as he patiently repairs the zip on his sports bag in which he has been rummaging. This engineering feat completed, he removes his odourless socks and takes a nap, his leg resting unselfconsciously against mine. When he awakens, he puts his socks back on, and, to my amazement, removes his baseball cap and then his T-shirt, the latter being swiftly replaced by a dark-coloured singlet that reveals not only more of the perfectly muscular arm but also the tattoo 'Airborne Alipio' in a winged motif just above the left bicep. AA then offers me some gum and tells me that he is flying from San Francisco to the Gay Games in New York where he is competing as a basketball player. This avowal explains the adroit but subtle exhibitionism he has so far displayed during the flight, an insight into his nature that is deepened by further remarks. So, he explains that the tattoo is a relic of days spent in the military, which may also account for the technical mastery in repairing the zip, and the meticulous orderliness of all his actions and kit, notwithstanding the confined space of the window seat in an airliner and the requirement to acknowledge, without undue imposition, the presence of an adjacent male.

6. Meeting a Delvaux Nude in Bern

A book I had written entitled *Paul Delvaux: Surrealizing the Nude* had just been published by a relatively new and soon-to-be successful London publisher. I had been asked by the editor to produce a monograph on a subject of my choice after the success a couple of years before of my previous book, an academic study, published by Cambridge University Press, centering on poetry and the visual arts in nineteenth-century France. The book had received an excellent review in *The Times Literary Supplement* and the new publisher was looking for promising authors. Since a concern of my book entitled *Pictorialist Poetics* had been in part, despite the onset of the avant-garde in mid-nineteenth-century France, the persistence of the academic tradition in French painting, I thought it might be interesting, in my new project, to explore further the work of the twentieth-century painter who continued to be inspired by this tradition more than any other, the Belgian Surrealist painter Paul Delvaux.

Although overshadowed by his famous contemporary René Magritte, I had been as struck by one of Delvaux's paintings – *Eloge de la Mélancolie* (1948) – as anything by Magritte – except perhaps for *Loving Perspective*, a picture that was in my text to provide an important parallel to another painting by Delvaux. I had also at this time been profoundly impressed by the Swiss critic and art historian Michel Thévoz who had, a decade before my monograph, published a remarkable study entitled *L'Académisme et ses fantasmes*. In this book, Thévoz argued that the continuance three centuries after Raphael of the conventionally mimetic or academic tradition in European art was the expression of a morbidly neurotic tendency: the apparently realistic and anatomically correct human figures, most often nude, enacting mythical roles, were, on an unconscious level, in fact invitations to the nineteenth-century male viewer (or one might say *voyeur*) to gain lewd or erotic pleasure while benefitting from the alibi that the paintings were merely representations of mythological subjects doing their time-honoured duty.

This heady mix of female nudity and a plausibly recognizable if not realistic context, clarified by Thévoz's psychoanalysis of what was, at a deeper level, at stake, provided me with the tools for a deeper investigation, in my book, of Delvaux's most characteristic works, which had been painted with an obsessive consistency throughout half a century of his life (from the 1930s to the 1980s). These works were large and carefully executed canvases, based on numerous drawings which were themselves often studies of the work of French academic predecessors such as Dominique Ingres, that almost invariably place a female nude (or nudes) in an apparently modern context, most often a railway station or tramline. In juxtaposing in a surrealist manner the mechanical modernity of transport or communication systems, with their rails and telegraph poles, with the tender curves of the female body, the painter seemed to want to release in his viewer (in particular male) unconscious fantasies of desire and penetration. The many fleeing (or 'loving') perspectives, the dark tunnels and erect or drooping railway signals, constituted a kind of sexual semaphore, an undisclosed climax being signaled by the imminent approach of some monster steam engine or line of tramcars.

An additional layer of erotic ambiguity was provided in such paintings as *Eloge de la Mélancolie* by Delvaux's use of incongruously modern electric lights within otherwise purely classical settings. These lamps simultaneously *indicated* the object of desire but also created shadows that could project as silhouettes from tangible objects forms inviting or demonstrating sexual arousal. So for example, in *Eloge de la Mélancolie*, the electric light above the classical statue of a male nude standing before the gaze of a naked female who in the foreground reclines invitingly in front of him (and the viewer), projects the outline of the scabbard of his sword as a shadow against the wall, creating the form of an erection that academic propriety as well as the marble figure's petrification would necessarily preclude from being enacted by the body itself.

The book that followed *Surrealizing the Nude* was a study of European stamp design that was to be accompanied by an exhibition in 1995–96 at the Design Museum in London. This book was a semiotic study that investigated the way some of the most sophisticated philatelic traditions in Europe – in particular, British, Dutch and Swiss – exploited the tension between the indexical and iconic properties of stamps as signs, and involved extensive research in the post offices and postal museums of several European capitals. While staying for this purpose for a few days in a hotel in Bern, I had an experience that was more vivid and erotic than any painting had ever provoked in me before.

On stepping one spring day from the hotel into the almost hallucinatory clarity of Bernese morning light, I was confronted by a vision more startling and disturbing than anything I'd ever seen, even in Delvaux: a beautiful and totally naked woman was slowly walking up the street in front of where I was standing on the hotel steps, followed at a respectful distance by a couple of policemen who seemed undecided as to the best way to handle this incidence of indecent exposure. The woman's facial expression was indescribable: it was both calm and yet apprehensive; her movements were both graceful and yet faintly inhibited; for an instant she made her nudity seem the most natural and beautiful thing in the world; and yet at the same time, she exuded an aura of transgression, provoking a feeling of profound unease. Before I could fully take in the impact of her apparition, she had disappeared round a corner, followed by the policemen whose heavy truncheons hung limp and useless from their black leather belts. It would have been indecent to follow, also counter-productive, for visions that are unfathomable are only experienced as a fleeting instant. It is the function of paintings to attempt to fix them, but only – as Delvaux seems to have understood – in such a way that they retain a certain impenetrability – one that is the price to be paid for ineffable desire.

I also reflected later on the chances of this event occurring: how often would an apparently sane and beautiful woman decide *in reality* to walk naked in broad daylight through the streets – and of a European capital city as staid as Bern? What were the odds on this event happening at the precise moment I happened to exit the hotel in which I was staying? Finally, what were the chances that one of the few privileged witnesses to this event should be myself in the role of author of a recent monograph on a painter – Paul Delvaux – whose speciality was precisely the depiction of female nudes walking as in a dream through a modern urban setting? Surreal is an adjective much misused as a descriptor of extraordinary events but in this case I think it applies with triple appropriateness: the event, the frame or pictorial intertext through which it was perceived (Delvaux's paintings), and the chance – or as the Surrealists would say, *le hasard objectif* – that brought these coincidences into synchronisation. No dream could have bettered this chance vision of the uncanny, brought to me so improbably on a weekday morning in Bern.

I discovered, subsequent to this chance happening, that the naked female walker had become quite notorious in northern Switzerland, having made a habit of exhibiting herself in this way in Zürich and other cities. This realization, however, hardly reduced the strangeness of the coincidence that led me to witness one of these walks at the time that I did and in the state of unconscious preparedness that my study of Delvaux's paintings had placed me. The combination of chances that brought it about remains therefore as much an object of wonder to me as the performance itself.

7. Getting Lost in Ratchadaphisek

Ratchadaphisek is a long avenue stretching north-south through the north-east part of Bangkok. It is a place where more recently established tourist hotels, massage parlours, supermarkets and shopping centres have superimposed themselves upon an older and more chaotic network of urban communities. The recent underground railway follows the road for most of its distance, punctuating its length with stations at Ratchadaphisek, Sutthisan, Huai Khwang and so on. Buses and taxis ply up and down the avenue, the latter famous for the U-turns ('U-turn' has become part of Thai vocabulary) that they have to practice to enable passengers to ascend on either side of the wide dual carriageway. In addition, there are several pedestrian bridges that offer both convenient crossing points and a vertiginous view of the adjacent neighbourhoods. And everywhere is to be seen, heard and smelt the swarm of mopeds that are the standard transport of Thai working people, as well as one of the cheapest and most convenient forms of taxi for single persons in a rush to travel a short distance.

The narrow and poorly maintained pavements that stretch along both sides of the dual carriageway are as eventful as the roadway itself. Punctuated by bus-stops, pedestrian bridges, underground railway entrances, hotel or shopping-centre forecourts, and the numerous junctions giving access to the many small 'soi' or alleys that branch off the main street, as much attention must be paid to deambulation along them as to driving in the jammed carriageways of the avenue. In addition, at certain junctions where older shopping areas meet new constructions, the pavement is invaded by local commerce with myriad stalls selling cheap goods, cigarettes, food and drink. The street restaurants indeed proliferate across the pavement, customers sitting down on tiny plastic stools to eat spicy dishes and sip beer in the heat and exhaust fumes of the Thai midday.

Pavements and footpaths are the surest indicator of the degree of civilisation of the urban centres in which they are found. So although a third-world city may impress by its spectacular skyline of high-rise hotels, skyscraper apartment blocks and shopping malls, if you cannot walk up the street without tripping over badly laid paving stones or unwonted obstacles, the city is not truly civilised. The great Brazilian city of São Paulo has one of the most impressive skylines in the southern hemisphere and many splendid streets and avenues. It has also inherited the wonderful Portuguese tradition, probably dating back to the Romans, of paving some of its sidewalks in complex tessellated patterns of black and white stone. So to walk up the Avenida Paulista is to perambulate a rhythmic op-art flow of pattern and texture. However, other streets in the city are not so fortunate: in the Rua Augusta, several kilometres long, the pavement varies according to the buildings that have their frontage along it: so the hapless walker may encounter classic tessellation, modern paving, decaying cement, AstroTurf, tarmacadam, gaping patches of red Brazilian earth, all within the same stroll.

The pavements of Bangkok are typically third-world in that they offer even in the most sophisticated and wealthy quarters of the city an only intermittently smooth passage: uneven paving slabs, absence of paving, decaying and rutted cement, the thoughtless intervention of countless dangerous obstacles (lamposts, footbridge stairs, sign posts, bus shelters), irregular curb height (where there is a curb at all), a temporary drainage pipe snaking its brown coils along the walk, all make perambulation treacherous. And that even before the habits and practices of other users is taken into account: the moped rider taking a short cut, the impromptu restaurant spreading its small stools across the passage, the taxi drivers swerving into hotel forecourts.

If Ratchadiphisek can seem a bit disorientating in the glare of tropical day, it becomes doubly labyrinthine when night descends on the city. I managed to get hopelessly lost in a short trip (one stop on the underground train – from Sutthisan to Huai Khwang) from the Veronika Hotel to the apartment of my friend Mark living in the Klangkrung condominium, situated a short way up Soi Nathong which branches off Ratchadaphisek on the same side as the Veronika near the Huai Khwang station. I had made the same trip in the daytime with no trouble and the return trip at night with similar ease, but managed on this occasion, by making one false move on exiting the underground station, to lose myself in a labyrinth from which only the beacon of the Emerald Hotel in conjunction with the Ariadne's ribbon of the mobile phone enabled me to extricate myself.

I got off the underground and exited confidently from the station, feeling already too much a habitué of Bangkok to check the way out I was following. I found myself next to the streaming traffic of Ratchadaphisek and looked for the nearby turn that would lead me directly to my destination. Off I set along the alley, navigating as best I could the broken pavement, cluttered with mopeds and stalls. I soon realized something was amiss when the shallow bridge over a small canal or drain did not appear to my left as anticipated. Realizing I must be walking up the wrong street, I about-turned and marched back to the subway exit. Here I telephoned my friend to ask for directions, the slightly peremptory tone of my enquiry suggesting the faintest irritation that he should be living in a place I could not easily find or that somehow he had conspired to re-configure the environs of his habitat. He suggested I climb on the back of a taxi moped, handing my phone to the driver so that he could give him the right directions. This I did but the driver

unfortunately did not understand the instructions and turfed
me off the back of his bike to give a better orientated customer
a lift. Mercifully, the other moped riders took pity on the gangly
blond *farang* and identified one of their number who would
deliver me to Soi Nathong. I gratefully climbed on the back of
the moped, clutching the driver round the waist (I was unaware
that the convention was to cling on to the bar at the back of the
saddle, not to the driver). The driver attempted to explain this
to me but with little success so he good-naturedly set off with
me hanging on to him.

After he had driven a few hundred metres up Ratchadaphisek,
I signaled to him to stop as I was sure he was heading in the
wrong direction. I dismounted and again telephoned my friend.
It was difficult to converse above the buzz of the busy motorway
and so I again placed myself at the mercy of the patient moped
driver. He insisted that Soi Nathong was at the *other side* of
the avenue, a situation that seemed inconceivable to me since I
was sure the alley was the same side as that which I exited the
subway. I therefore paid off the moped driver and began to look
for a sign of orientation. It was then that I saw the gleaming
facade of the Emerald Hotel, rising like a beacon on the *opposite
side* of the avenue. It was only then that I realized that, far from
the urban geography changing its orientation to confound me,
I had somehow got myself on the wrong side of the road.

I then walked along to the nearest footbridge which I crossed
with vaguely reckless thoughts and from there located the Soi
I was looking for. But my problems were not yet over. I again
phoned my patient friend Mark who gave me directions as to
the turn-off into his condo. But once again, the noise of the
street interfered with the directions and I managed to walk the
length of the alley missing the well-signposted right turn. By
this time, I was in a state of near despair and so put in yet
another call. My friend was by now, I imagine, understandably
losing patience and instead of, as I secretly hoped, coming

out to meet me, merely repeated the directions he had already given. So I set off again and within a minute miraculously found myself staring at the entry to the condo, shining like a pink El Dorado in the gloom. I promptly marched in, the small labyrinth that the development constituted being relatively easy to negotiate after the travails of the preceding forty minutes. And so I arrived, exhausted and bathed in sweat, as if after a long and dangerous trek through alien territory, scarcely in a state to enjoy the planned pleasures of the evening – an hour in the gym before a splash in the pool and then drinks on the balcony. The cause of my disorientation was soon identified: the exit to the right side of Ratchadiphisek is to be found by turning right and *doubling back* inside the station before mounting the stairs to exit, a turn that in my impatience or over-confidence I had missed, so giving myself one of those hours of sweat and confusion that retrospectively become the part of the pleasure of living in Bangkok.

8. Flash Flood in Udon Thani

Travelling upcountry in Thailand tends to be a mixed pleasure. One leaves the smog and humidity of Bangkok's shapeless sprawl looking forward to the lush green vegetation, the country-fresh food and the artless welcome of the provinces' inhabitants. At the same time one dreads the unpicturesque ramshackle of the ill-defined town centres, the uneasy mix of tradition and modernity, the damp-stained cement of the walls, the already ruinous state of half-completed concrete pavements and the islands of rubbish swilled by tropical showers into half-blocked drains or swirled into unimaginable landscapes in the middle of the street.

There is also the question of the best way to travel out of Bangkok: a railway trip, often slowed by unscheduled stops or delays, but during which the traveller has time to adjust to the different rhythm and environment of provincial Thailand, setting out in daylight knowing that the tropical night will already have descended by the time of arrival; or the rapid but banal internal flight that delivers the passenger within an hour or two to the different world of the remoter province. Both modes of transport have disadvantages but on the occasion recounted here, a scheduled flight managed to submit its passengers to vicissitudes not normally encountered by rail or air.

The flight took off promptly enough, the aircraft climbing into a darkening sky but continuing undaunted on its way through thunderous-looking clouds and occasional flashes of lightning. The air-hostess's smile scarcely wavered as she delivered the usual safety instructions and then refreshments to the passengers, most of whom were settled to what they presumed would be a short and uneventful trip. And indeed, after an hour or so, the aircraft began its descent on schedule through the rain to the airport at Udon Thani. The descent, however, did not, as expected, complete itself as a landing, but suddenly turned into a climb as the main runway and airfield below, visible in glimpses between the grey vapour that scudded past the windows, began to recede. Passengers stared uneasily ahead, some focusing on the impassible expression of the air-hostesses facing them who were duly buckled into their seats. Why had the aircraft not landed at the appointed destination, one that was clearly visible and seemingly unobstructed? Passengers had to wait a few tense moments, tied up in their anxious conjectures, before it was announced by the pilot that on making the landing approach he became aware that the runway was awash to a depth that it would have been unsafe for him to land on. The flight would therefore return to Bangkok and await news of improved conditions that might enable a second attempt at landing in Udon Thani later in the evening.

So the by now frayed nerves of the passengers sitting again in the departure lounge of the main airport at Bangkok, were submitted to a further test as the flight awaited clearance to re-commence its itinerary and eventually deliver the air travellers to their destination. This it did after a couple of hours' wait and, at the second attempt, the aircraft duly landed at Udon Thani airport, still glistening in the rain but no longer submerged beneath the recent flash flood.

On exiting the airport, myself and my two friends, Mark, an Irishman, and Matthew, an American, quickly resolved to make up for lost time by heading for a bar to slake our thirst and our mild sense of relief in a few beers before setting out to a much recommended traditional Thai restaurant just outside the town. The three tall and hungry men thus soon after found themselves squeezed into the back of a cycle rickshaw that splashed its way through the puddles of the rutted streets of Udon Thani towards the hoped-for destination in the darkness.

After twenty or so cramped minutes, the rickshaw wobbled to a halt in a country lane outside a dark and what proved, alas, to be a shut-up building, the restaurant being closed that night. As the three disconsolate westerners descended from the rickshaw to stretch for a moment in their damp white T-shirts in the shining darkness, a hapless fish chose that instant to attempt to flap its way across the narrow rain-soaked road from one monsoon ditch to the other: three quarters of the way across, however, a moped suddenly appeared out of the darkness in a trajectory that brought it into exact collision course with the hapless vertebrate.

Snorting with mixed amusement and pity at the unappetizing spectacle, Matthew, Mark and myself clambered back into the cramped cabin of the rickshaw and were bumped back into Udon-Thani in the hope of safely reaching a destination that would provide nourishment of a more satisfying kind than that of the fish whose untoward end we had just witnessed.

9. Hanoi Pickpockets

Since the onset of sexual tourism in South-East Asia, developing in particularly from the 1960s when, during the Vietnam War, American servicemen would during their periods of leave regularly seek sex with young women – or sometimes young men – in Bangkok or other towns in Thailand (one of the few countries in that part of Asia not torn by violent political or ideological strife), the foreign (and in particular Western) male has become a common focus or target of sexual propositioning, whether or not he happens to be seeking such attention. In Thailand, it is almost impossible for a lone male in a bar, restaurant or commercial area to remain so for long, since within the Thai ethos, a person on their own cannot be happy, and leaving them in such a state would be a breach of natural Thai hospitality.

The normalizing since the turn of the century of female- as well as male-activated sexual commerce, in Vietnam, Laos, and Cambodia, as well as in Thailand, has somewhat complicated – some might say enriched – *farang* / native interaction, leading the visitor to those countries, in particular the male tourist, to be more attentive to the reading of signs, in particular those expressed through human body language. For other vices such as robbery, most frequently in the form of pickpocketing – as commonly practiced by women as by men – often operate under the cover of sexual enticement. So when a *farang* male is greeted by a woman or small group of women by the standard greeting 'You handsome' he should be as attentive to his wallet, watch and mobile phone as to his sexual parts.

The truth of this was brought home to me in Hanoi on a visit to Vietnam with my friend Mark a few years ago.

The assault on the senses – smell and touch as well as sight and sound – central Hanoi provides to its foreign visitors is one of its most unforgettable attributes. As is also the initial (mis-)apprehension of Vietnam's capital as a demonstration of organized chaos. For this is a city in which the line between inside and outside, private and public, intimate and commercial, is very faintly drawn. The visiting foreigner or *farang* has thus quickly to abandon his reliance on western categories of social apprehension or expectation and adjust rapidly to a complex and constantly moving situation.

Life is primarily lived in Hanoi – as a family or as a commercial enterprise – on the pavement, so the visitor will within one street or alley find himself stepping over a family meal, a display of recently butchered meat, the disassembled components of a motor bike, a colourful display of tee-shirts, boxer shorts and other underwear, an exhibition of ironmongery, a vegetable stall or a barber's shop. So the smell of raw meat, hair oil, motor lubricant, fresh beans or simmering soup will simultaneously strike the senses while the necessity to watch where one is placing one's feet and to steer a safe passage through the miscellaneous throng makes even a leisurely stroll an adventure. And this is not counting attempting to cross the street, a daring undertaking since it means negotiating an unending and unregulated stream of mopeds, all of which seem to be set on collision course with the hapless pedestrian.

At night, the pavements are not quite so encumbered but the thoroughfares themselves seem even more crazily congested with hooting and swerving mopeds delivering not only their riders but also their pillion-passengers to the many clubs, bars, restaurants, massage parlours and other places of sometimes dubious repute that enrich South-East Asian nightlife. One of the first things a *farang* does on arrival in Hanoi is to find – or more likely be found by – a willing bike-rider who will attach himself to you the duration of your visit and be always on hand to deliver you to whatever destination within the city you choose. He will also wait – sometime for hours – outside a restaurant or club until you emerge and is ready at any time to take you where you want to go. My friend Mark and I had quickly been identified by a likely pair of such bikers on our first evening out in Hanoi and were safely and cheerfully transported by them at a very fair rate throughout the rest of our stay in the city.

It was one night while they were waiting patiently for Mark and myself to emerge from a bar that I experienced the strange encounter that was to lose me my new mobile phone. Within the bar where we had been slaking our tropical thirst on numerous beers, I seemed already to have been identified by a pair of Thai women as ripe for dispossession; for, on exiting, blinking in the darkness, I was immediately accosted by the (in my case probably ironic) chorus of 'You handsome' and before I knew what was happening having my sexual parts explored by female fingers. I was so busy trying to fend off the unsolicited interest in my balls of the first woman that I did not notice the hands of the second slip into my jeans pocket and remove my phone. At that moment, our two faithful bike boys came to the rescue, scaring off the women, and Mark and I took the seat behind our riders to make a speedy escape to the night's next destination, a dance club at the other side of the city. It was only on exiting that joint a couple of hours later that I noticed the absence of bulge in my right jeans pocket and realized that I had been relieved of my phone. Such, however, are the delights of Hanoi that the mishap was soon written off to experience. Hot damn, it's Vietnam.

10. Saigon Cycle Rickshaw Ride

If Hanoi is, under western eyes, organized chaos, Saigon appears somewhat more ordered, perhaps since European or American influence has imparted a more familiar logic to some aspects of the way things are done. However, this interaction of ethoses can lead to a different kind of cultural misunderstanding, as my friend Mark and I were to discover in 2007 on flying down from Hanoi to Saigon for a few days. We were then to learn that there were in many aspects of Saigon life two parallel modes of operation: for tourist transport – bicycle rickshaws as well as mopeds or regular motor taxis; for eating places – European style restaurants or off-the-pavement stalls. In addition to this was the pan-Vietnamian subtropical quasi simultaneity of different types of weather – hot and brilliant sunshine and torrential rain – to which the natives seemed instantaneously to adapt. And of course, the tall blondish *farang* male stood out in sharp contrast to his shorter, darker South-East Asian counterpart.

Setting out from our hotel the first morning, in view of the hot and humid weather, clad merely in singlets and shorts, Mark and I were only half way down the street towards the centre of town when overtaken by torrential rain. We dived for cover beneath the awning of a stall but were almost immediately identified by a pair of bicycle rickshaw riders who had evidently spotted us for what in effect we were – easy tourist prey. Mark began to negotiate with one of the riders while I shivered under the dripping awning of the stall and before I knew what was happening I was bundled into the front compartment of a cycle rickshaw and soon being bumped to an as yet undisclosed destination. The trip was pretty hair-raising as the bike-boy blundered through the ruts of the road, swerving to avoid the motorized traffic that seemed to pass mere inches away from the fragile structure of the rickshaw. The rain, as well as seeping through the leaking canvas roof, was also splashing up from the puddles so that, soaked to my boxers, I felt like a mop being sluiced in a bucket inches deep in water.

Eventually the rickshaws clattered to a halt and we clambered from them into a large open-fronted restaurant where we were to take breakfast. Instead of departing after their delivery, however, our two bike-riders took it upon themselves to join us and use the opportunity to negotiate possible future services to us as we ate our eggs and fried rice. Part of the potential contract included, as well as regular delivery to whatever destination we chose in Saigon during our stay, the sexual availability of the women who were serving us in the café. The boys' overtures were supported by a bundle of glowing references supplied by previous European tourist clients, including photographs. The rickshaw riders' rapidly advancing familiarity with us extended to quite personal comments on our appearance, in particular the question of my age: although I was much older than Mark, I was dressed in similarly minimal way and my bare shoulders and arms were still quite smoothly muscular – not least since at this time I was competing seriously as a boxer and training intensively, with Mark as my chief sparring partner; this made me seem younger than I was – a conundrum that seemed insoluble to our putative Vietnamese protectors.

At this point, the sun was beginning to re-emerge from behind the steely-grey storm clouds and I hinted to Mark that this would be a good moment to make a dash for freedom: finish your beer and run, I whispered. This we did, but only to the momentary astonishment of the two rickshaw lads who were soon back on their bikes and following us down the street, assailing us with further blandishments with respect to the many services they could still offer. We eventually shook them off and by the time we reached the city centre, our shorts dried out and the sun beginning to burn our bare shoulders, we were ready to find one of the French restaurants for which Saigon is still famous and enjoy a meal undistracted by unwanted solicitations, however well intentioned.

11. Visa Run to Vientiane

Farangs with only tenuous employment in Bangkok or with plans for the immediate future in Thailand not fully decided, often find themselves suddenly towards the end of the standard three-month visitor time allowance. This means the hasty booking of a flight out to a city in a bordering country from whence they can return to Thailand with a visa duly renewed. The most convenient of these temporary destinations include Chang-Mai, on the Burmese border, or Vientiane, capital of Laos, sited on a stretch of the Mekong River that divides it from Thailand.

For some reason – timing or anticipated expense – my Bangkok-based friend Mark, with whom I was staying, opted to do the Vientiane run, by *train*. Far from being an exotic adventure, though, the rail trip turned out to be lengthy, tedious and slow. Although the journey was only a couple of hundred miles, owing to the parlous state of the track, it took a whole night to complete. Encumbered with the lightest possible of rucksacks and equipped in anticipation with a bottle of whiskey and a large bag of ice, Mark and I installed ourselves in our bunks and waited for the train to lurch into movement. Since it was an eight p.m. departure, it was already night when we pulled out of the station, so darkness veiled the endless shacks and shanties that straggle for miles along the metropolitan stretch of the track. The railway carriages, at least half a century old, were of the side-corridor type, interconnected tenuously by concertina-like passages. The jacks were simple in the extreme, with a squatter-type shithole and a urinal that required careful aim as the carriage constantly lurched and swayed. However, the whiskey worked its magic sufficiently for some sleep to be had, despite intermittent interruption by jolts that sometimes foretold long intervals of complete standstill.

The shattering effect of long journeys by land or by air was felt in the usual way on arrival at the Thai border, despite – or maybe in part because of – the bright morning light and sudden rise in temperature. Also by the realization that arrival at the frontier was only the beginning of the operation: riders of cycle rickshaws jostled to capture the custom of the *farang* arrivals and transport them to a shack where motor transport to the frontier itself (only a couple of kilometers distant) could be bartered. On delivery to the border checkpoint, passports had to be produced to cross the frontier and then a similar mechanism played out in reverse as the best deal for transport to Vientiane, several kilometers away, across the long bridge spanning the simmering River Mekong, had to be negotiated. So a sense of tension and alienation added to the fatigue of the operation, the heat of the tropical climate compounding both the psychological and physical sweat of negotiating legal passage. And arrival in Vientiane was not the happy end of the story as the relevant embassy or consulate then had to be located and the hours for visa renewal ascertained and planned for.

With this eventually achieved, that moment, often overlooked but nevertheless one of the most blissful of long-distance travel, came when it became possible to peel off the crumpled shirt and shorts that carried the odour of two days wearing, and step into a cleansing shower from which to re-emerge refreshed and with a renewed appetite for both food and living. Also the possibility of a massage and several cooling beers in an unfamiliar environment that was re-exoticized, even re-eroticized, by the sense of mission at least in part accomplished.

Marking time between the crucial appointed hour of passport renewal and the moment of departure for the frontier post to re-enter the country that only the day before had been exited, was also one of mixed pleasure and anxiety. Vientiane, given its colonial past, is not short of cafés and restaurants catering to both local and European tastes and its importance as a trading centre is evident in the colossal centre-city bazaar selling all kinds of exotic foods and fabrics. The necessity of travelling light and the anxiety about customs duties prevented, however, full benefit from being taken of the tantalizing availability of rare merchandise, so once again it was the immediate satisfaction of human well-being that became the dominant but ephemeral priority. Far eastern countries seem to provide for this need perhaps more fully and comprehensively than any other part of the world, so that the *souvenir* of the passage through an Asian country is integrated into the physical body, like a spicy flavour on the tongue, as much as externalized in the form of gratuitous objects. Perhaps in the light of this, such institutions as the national military/historical museum in Vientiane, while offering an extraordinary display of weapons and army hardware, and some elaborate and proportionately outmoded ideological sculptures, provide not even the most minimal documentation: no postcards were available to attest to proof of passage, only sunburnt limbs and a memorably fierce thirst: the display is largely open air, and, except for a couple of nonchalant soldier guards, completely deserted.

The return to Thailand the following day was a re-enactment in reverse of the business of departure only twenty or thirty hours previously, with the added anxiety of ensuring that the newly acquired visa be correctly stamped with the three-month date permit. The return overnight journey to Bangkok was as tedious as the outgoing, complicated by the nearest onboard lavatory being hopelessly blocked, and impoverished by the lack of a bottle of whiskey to help anaesthetize the boredom of the trip. The sun was already up when the train eventually rattled and shuddered its way into Bangkok the following morning so that the dirty picturesque (as Richard Burton would have categorized it in his patronizing nineteenth-century insouciance) of the slums following the track was fully apparent. An hour's taxi ride through the dynamic chaos of the Bangkok morning was the final trial to be endured before a further refreshing shower, change of clothes and long siesta marked the end of the visa run mission.

12. Biking over the Back of an Elephant

Ko Chang (or Elephant Island) is perhaps the most picturesque and least spoilt of all the Thai islands in the Gulf of Siam. It may be this in part because it is quite difficult of access: it is far too steep for any airport and the ferry-crossing from the mainland in south-east Thailand, though short, is difficult of access. My Thai-based friend Mark and I had to take a long overnight trip in a taxi from Bangkok to get to the ferry port, a trip made messier by Mark's insistence that he bring with us in the back of the taxi Tupperware boxes containing some of the nourishing soups he had been concocting for lunch while we were in Bangkok. These sat on the floor of the taxi, but with the lurching of the vehicle one of them spilt so that for the rest of the ride our flip flop-clad feet were slipping around in a centimetre of liquid as we breathed in the sickening odour of damp carpet mixed with spicy soup, rendered more nauseous still by the taxi driver's cigarette smoke. On arrival at the Thai coast at about midnight, it was difficult to find accommodation before the next sailing the following morning. In the end we were obliged to settle for a couple of mosquito-infested huts half way up the side of a hill and to accept a lift to the ferry boat the next day squashed into the front of a truck.

However, as soon as the ferry chugged off, the magic of Ko Chang became apparent: from the sea, it seemed beyond its white sandy beaches to be totally wooded, with very little sign of human life and even less of tourist activity. The island is very hilly, and the narrow road that hugs its western shore offers a roller-coaster ride. Transport to the chalets we had booked took the form of a char-à-banc, onto the roof of which our luggage

was summarily thrown; it was a miracle that it survived the
twists, turns and steep climbs of the route down the coast. The
other passengers in the back of the truck gave a foretaste of
the mix of *farang* visitors to be expected: a pair of gay London
males regaling us with a display of bitching and banter, two
loud Russians, and a young French couple whose sophistication
was unruffled by the scene. However, once they successively
alighted, these visitors were never seen again and after thirty
minutes, Mark and I were disgorged in a village and soon settled
into a pair of chalets on the hillside overlooking the coast.

The condominium was beautifully landscaped with clumps
of palms and tropical flowering plants enlivened by the chatter of
colourful birds. Water trickled down narrow courses following
the pathways. The chalets' balconies faced the coast and in the
evening offered vivid views of sunsets through the trees, while
their ceilings were the scene of endlessly watchable displays
of tiny salamanders pouncing on their insect prey. The at first
disconcerting trumpeting that came from the neighbouring
terrain was soon identified as that of the elephants after which
the island it seems was named and which were kept there in a
little patch of jungle.

Transport around the island was either by motorbike or
bicycle. Mark and I mostly used the former but on one hot day
manfully decided to cycle to one of the chief attractions of the
island, a relatively remote waterfall that gushed its stream into
a basin shaded by dense foliage. Even with a full set of gears it
was impossible to cycle up all the hills so sometimes we had
to dismount, and the descents around sharp bends were often
hair-raising. The reward for an hour's strain and sweat, however,
was to slip naked into the cooling waters of a natural rock pool
under the green penumbra of branches.

The motorbike option, though less testing physically, was
no less challenging as, apart from one long straight stretch
connecting two straggling villages, the island consisted mostly

of steep rises and tortuous descents: the grey and wrinkled surface of the roads was strangely like that of an elephant's skin while the sensations of bike-rider and pillion as they swayed in tandem or were thrown against each other as the bike negotiated the twists and turns of the route, were akin to what I imagined it must be like sitting on the back of an elephant ambling across uneven terrain.

Part II   Boxing Rings

1. A Corner of the Playground

My first boxing encounter was as a ten-year-old schoolboy, when my schoolmates, fed up with knuckle-bones and leap-frog, began to look for excitement in less childish forms of competition. Each boy, if he did not himself possess them, would borrow a pair of boxing gloves from a dad or elder brother, and a ring was improvised in the corner of the schoolyard. Two orange-boxes marked the 'corners' and a referee/time-keeper was appointed from among the group. Boys selected themselves into opposing pairs, a motley selection of gloves of all sizes and colours were laced on, and the fights began. The competitions were ragged and chaotic and as often ended in collapse before the time-keeper needed to call the end of the round. The competing boys sank onto their stools with relief, their battered and badly laced gloves already coming adrift, as grubby handkerchiefs were fluttered in their faces to cool them down. Victory in each bout was decided at the first show of blood or when one boxer broke down in tears or exhaustion. The first punch on the nose I received was a disturbing sensation – yet the rush of adrenaline as well as of blood gave rise to a surprising feeling of self-assurance as well as vulnerability. The winners were distributed with chewing-gum cards showing the current champions: I lost my bout to a thick-set boy whom I envied for the possession of a card showing Floyd Patterson, current heavyweight champion of the world. To me, with his smooth caramel-coloured skin and psycho-billy haircut, Patterson was the most glamorous male on the planet.

When the following year, as part of the eleven-plus examination, I was obliged to write a composition on 'Playground Games', the schoolyard boxing skirmishes suggested themselves as a plausible topic. In this way, though I did not realize it then, my hasty essay on the subject became the first of many efforts on my part to express in writing boxing's strange appeal.

2. Schoolboy Boxing

At the grammar school I went to, boxing was part of physical training, or PT. It was taught in the school gym that seemed on first acquaintance a strange and awe-inspiring space: enclosed in wooden wall-bars, it was littered with exotic equipment: suede-covered bucks and vaulting-horses, the strangely named medicine balls, ropes and collapsible wooden gates suspended from the ceiling. At the end, in pride of place, a boxing ring raised eighteen inches above the ground. Before acceding to this space, boys had to climb into their white cotton gym shorts or black satin boxing trunks in a drafty changing room. Boxing gloves – old and wrinkled in prune-coloured leather – were stored in a cupboard. Training proceedings commenced with a programme of circuits comprising press-ups, squats, burpees, routines with the medicine ball, jumps on and off low wooden benches, and shadow-boxing. When the real action commenced, pairs of skinny boys clad only in singlets, gym shoes and creased satin shorts – there were no head-guards, gum-shields or abdominal protectors – climbed into the ring for three two-minute rounds. Though there were plenty of flurries of punches, and the occasional shot was landed, most of the ordeal consisted in trying to keep one's fists up and one's chin down, to bounce out of trouble along the flexible trapezoid of the ropes, and to avoid collapsing with exhaustion before the bell clanged at the end of the third round. The adrenaline rush at the end of each bout was quickly counteracted by a brisk warm-down, a cold shower and a hasty change back into school uniform in the drafty changing room. The pleasure of retrospective analysis – 'You nearly got

me with your left in the second'; 'If you'd stuck it out a second
longer, I'd have been finished', etc – could only be indulged in
the break after training, before heading back to classes at which
it was difficult to concentrate on the work in hand.

3.   Trinity College Dublin Gym

The Trinity College gym of the 1990s and 2000s was approached
up a narrow staircase that ran up beside the boat-club house.
The boxing room was barely twenty-foot square, one corner
being further eaten into by a toilet and shower cubicle. The four-
teen-foot ring, mounted directly on the floor, barely fitted into
the remaining space in which there was just room for a floor-to-
ceiling punch-ball and a heavy bag, plus a cupboard in which
gloves and other vital boxing equipment was stored. The smell
of the room was the usual pleasant admixture of bruised leather,
sweat and grubby canvas; the atmosphere was warmed with ex-
ercising human bodies and two wall-mounted electric heaters.
Up to a dozen and a half student boxers would crowd into the
space after an hour's preparatory training in the much larger
Sports Hall situated a hundred metres away. Hand-wraps were
quickly wound round fists, gloves, head-guards and abdominal
protectors put on, and the group divided up into approximately
matching weight categories ready for sparring.

Proceedings were presided over by our trainer, Dan, a
mythical figure, a former Irish international heavyweight boxer,
who was held in awe and respect by every member of the club.
Four roughly matched boxers would climb into the ring to be
exposed in pairs to rounds of hard sparring at a minute or two
a turn. Dan's encouragement, cajoling and criticisms would
be loudly articulated and there was never a moment when
the situation, though often rough, was allowed to get out of
hand. One sometimes waited in dread to be called to confront

a member of the group, perhaps a southpaw or thrower of haymakers, whom one knew would give one a hard time. The more promising boxers were exhorted to exert themselves, Dan being unsparing in his criticisms of their failings – tactical or positional. More than usually severe or heavy blows he greeted with a deep chortle, the proceedings coming to an end when he announced in a gruff diminuendo: 'Shake hands'. The intimacy of the place, the spirit of camaraderie among the young boxers, the sense of authenticity lent by the presence of a trainer who was a genuine ex-professional, the total commitment of all concerned to the tussles in hand, combined to create an experience that was for me the essence of college boxing.

4.   First Fight in New York: Gleason's Gym

Gleason's Gym is probably the most famous boxing gym in the world, the training place of American champions, the home of white-collar boxing and a place to which boxers regardless of age, gender, race or colour naturally gravitate. It has had several sites in the city but is currently ensconced under Brooklyn Bridge, at the New York City end. Four rings are contained within its compact confines, a quarter of which are eaten into by spartan changing rooms and a small shop selling boxing gear. The dominant impression is one of frenetic activity as boxers simultaneously skip, lift weights, punch heavy bags, flick speed-balls, shadow-box, spar or generally lounge about observing the proceedings. The fighters are dressed in sweat-stained hoodies, beaten up boxing boots, grubby satin shorts, some wearing the classic Gleason's T-shirt with its proud Virgilian motto emblazoned on the back: 'Now, whoever has courage and a strong and collected spirit in his breast, let him come forward, lace on the gloves and put up his hands'.

My experience of the gym was more than usually poignant since I was there to train in the run-up to my first white-collar fight, scheduled for a couple of days later in the Trinity Gym in downtown New York. (White collar boxing is a version of the sport organised for men over the thirty-five-year age limit that governs regular amateur boxing). Back from a few days training camp in the Catskill Mountains with other members of the Irish white-collar boxing team, I was disgorged with my training bag and my fellow fighters from a white stretch limo and told to strip in preparation for a spar with a young Columbian boxer named Emilio Roorhaus. I was in an agony of nervous anticipation as I repaired to the drafty changing room to climb into my Kelly-green boxing trunks, trimmed with blue, and marked with my fighting name 'Dynamo'. It was the same anxiety I had felt as a schoolboy and as a college boxer stepping into the charted but always unknown territory that is the boxing ring. In the event the spar with the young Columbian was not a testing experience since he was much shorter than I and was being exhorted by his trainer to aim body blows at me. I was therefore easily able to pick him off with my long left jab and the occasional follow-up right hook to the head. I was so taken aback by the ease with which I dominated the situation that the whole event seemed unreal, a state of confusion enhanced by the constant flow of conflicting advice offered by the onlookers crowding round the ring and aimed at either boxer. It took a cold shower after the bout to bring back a sense of reality and temporarily to relieve the anxiety that had infiltrated my pleasure in lacing on the gloves in this mythic boxing space.

5.   Training in the National Stadium Dublin

If the boxing ring may be reckoned among the most disturbing yet alluring spaces in modern culture, to step into such a space at the national headquarters of the sport is a specially challenging experience. As a white-collar boxer, I trained regularly in the gym at the National Stadium in Dublin where I was teamed up to spar with a motley collection of aspiring fighters of all ages and sizes: builders, shopkeepers, civil servants. It was remarkable how quickly we all adapted to the discipline of boxing training though the lessons we learnt on the floor of the gym were seldom translated into elegant or efficient action in the ring. Some of the bigger men would propel themselves at their opponents like meteors at a planet, fists flying but seldom contacting. Others, more measured, would duck and weave, the full size of the stadium training ring giving a heightened sense of both the space and the loneliness of the fight encounter.

I remember thinking I had the mastery of one short but pugnacious contestant, clouting him with a right hook that knocked his head-protector askew. However, he very soon countered with a sledgehammer right to my head that was so sharp that it caused the message 'Why am I doing this?' to be relayed in a flash across my mind. Part of the strangeness of boxing, however, lies in the speed with which one recovers composure after an unsettling blow: stars are literally seen for a second but with a disbelieving shake of the head, the mind becomes focused again and is already intent on reciprocating the hurt and humiliation it has just experienced. The toughest part of boxing is not so much receiving the blows, which, however heavy and unsettling, come wrapped in up to sixteen ounces of padded leather and so have some of their impact muffled; it is rather the determination, especially in a close contest, to make the extra effort to win the fight, and not to settle for the softer option of moving out of trouble even at the expense of losing the decision. In the end, boxing is all about stamina and willpower, both of which have to be stretched to their limit if one is to emerge victorious from an evenly matched bout. At least, that's the lesson I felt I'd learnt in the Dublin National Stadium ring.

6. Garden Boxing

Boxing can quickly become an obsession and the enthusiast finds himself sizing up various unlikely sites as settings for possible future pugilistic action. Having designed at home a fifteen-foot square conservatory that would double as a boxing gym (high enough for a centrally suspended heavy bag and with room a for a floor-to-ceiling ball), a natural complement seemed to be a nearby corner of the garden where a cabbage palm, a cherry tree, a fig tree and a wooden post demarcated an approximately twenty-foot square. Fenced off with blue rope, the space became a boxing ring which in the summer could be used for sparring. The lawn on which it is set is not the most even and in more violent flurries the hapless boxer might find himself propelled into a raspberry bed or a clump of rhododendron, but the rustic charm of the space more than makes up for these deficiencies. It is also interesting to see how quickly the central part of the turf square is worn into a dusty ring, marking the trajectory of the boxers as they circle each other in search of an opening.

The highlight of the summer is when the College boxing club come back to train in this space: the usual circuits involving bags, punch-balls, skipping and press-ups are accommodated in and around the conservatory; then the sparring ensues in the improvised ring. Boxing in its modern form (as indeed in its ancient origins) was of course conceived as an outdoor sport: eighteenth-century English fighters set to on a patch of turf surrounded by a *circle* of enthusiastic observers, many of whom were betting on the outcome of the match. The *ring* only became squared later in the century when for reasons of crowd management and clarity of observation, the square of turf became marked off by posts linked by ropes. The two boxers met in the centre of the 'ring' which was marked by a 'scratch', a point from which each new round recommenced after a fall by one of the contestants. Since on and off over the eighteenth and nineteenth centuries boxing was, like cockfighting, an illegal activity, rings had to be quickly improvised and as swiftly taken down. So, some of the pleasures of improvising a boxing ring outside derives from its historic antecedents in the pugilistic tradition and the sense of transgression as well as of risk that accompanies the sport.

7.   Gypsy Ring

The transgressive principle as well as the danger associated with boxing are to be felt all the more keenly in the most outlandish fight setting I have ever seen, that of a secret ring constructed by Travellers on a hillside in a remote pine forest near the foothills of the Wicklow Mountains. One cold winter afternoon in 2006, Paddy (captain of the Trinity boxing club), Mark (captain of cricket and a sparring partner) and myself set off to locate this magical site of rustic pugilism which was a few kilometers up the hillside from Paddy's home near Kilternan. A tough jog up the steep and narrow lines in the vicinity of the old lead mines, with its gaunt helter-skelter tower, eventually brought us to the dense pine wood in which the ring was concealed. The closeness of the trees and the steepness of the slope made me skeptical of ever finding the site but it was soon discovered: a space between four trees in an almost exactly square configuration had been roped off, and a level platform built to counteract the slope on which the ring was sited. A rough tarpaulin served as a canvas covering the branches of the floor of the ring, itself further softened by a fine layer of pine needles. The corner posts were padded with rubbish bags stuffed with old clothes. The waning winter light flickered wanly through the gaps between the trees as we sat on a couple of benches roughly hewn from felled pine trunks for a few minutes contemplating this magical space. Had it not been so cold and had we not been, boxers all, ashamedly *afraid* that the returning Travellers might discover us and initiate a combat we might prefer not to engage in, we might have stripped off there and then and, like eighteenth-century pugilists in their breeches, set to with bare knuckles in the invigorating fresh air laced with the pungent smell of pine.

8.   Boxing on the Fo'c's'le of RMS St Helena

Boxing is an addictive as well as an obsessive sport and, as any hardened practitioner will tell you, anxiety and boredom set in if even a few days pass without some boxing activity figuring in the weekly routine. In 2003 I had the chance to take a four-week boat trip from England to South Africa, including a week's stopover on the South Atlantic island of St Helena. I was sailing on the RMS St Helena, half cargo boat, half passenger liner, that regularly plied the length of the North and South Atlantic. As it is usual on boat trips where there are numerous passengers, deck games were regularly organised – deck cricket, table-tennis, quoits – but these amusements did not satisfy my need for the more challenging training required for boxing. There was a minuscule gym on board – just room for a cycling machine and an exercise mat – where I set myself a daily routine of hundred press-ups, a task made trickier by the rolling of the ship as it ploughed through the Atlantic surge.

Luckily there was just one other user of the gym, a hefty and bearded South African called Wolf. After a few days sweating in the gym together, I persuaded Wolf to vary his routine with some skipping and shadow-sparring on the fo'c's'le of the St Helena, a square space situated against the ship's funnel above the upper deck. Approached by a metal gangway and surrounded by railings, unfrequented by other passengers aboard, the space formed an ideal training area for boxing. A length of ship's rope served for skipping exercises, after which Wolf and myself set to:

clad only in swimming trunks and training mitts, the bronzed bodies of the two of us learnt to compensate for the surging and listing of the ship as we circled each other, throwing routine shadow punches. The freshness of the air, the smell of salt, the exhilaration of moving around in such an unstable space, gave us a hearty appetite and a healthy thirst, both of which were duly slaked afterwards in the ship's excellent restaurant and bar. If the RMS St Helena had been a naval ship ('RMS' stands for 'Royal Mail Ship'), there would no doubt have been the possibility of improvising a proper ring, boxing traditionally being a favourite sport in the Senior Service, given that it is one of the few that can be accommodated within the narrow confines of a ship's deck.

9.   Bare-knuckle Boxing

It is a common misconception that bare-knuckle boxing is more dangerous or painful than boxing with gloves. The misleading phrase 'taking the gloves off', used to signify a no-holds-barred confrontation, does not necessarily apply in boxing. This is because, as George Bernard Shaw and others recognized over a century ago, the compulsory use of gloves in amateur and professional boxing did not in any way alleviate the impact of punches delivered. On the contrary, the advantage of the glove is not only, as its inventor John Broughton said in 1743, to 'avoid the Inconvenience of Bloody Noses', but also, in protecting the fist, to enable far heavier and more frequent punches to be thrown without damage to the boxer doing the throwing. So the glove is there primarily to protect the hitter, not the hit. Late eighteenth- and early nineteenth-century pugilists were able to endure scores of rounds of bare-knuckle boxing whereas today a pair of super-fit heavyweight boxers would be unlikely to survive beyond the current twelve-round limit if either of them knew their business.

This fact, however, does little to detract from the appeal of bare-knuckle boxing which every pugilist at some stage or another, if only fleetingly, dreams of practicing at least once. (Chuck Palahniuk's novel *Fight Club* undoubtedly captures an important part of the appeal of such bare-knuckle encounters.) This appeal is in part fuelled by a certain nostalgia for those Regency days when a man would strip to his breeches for a set-to in an open-air, and often illegal, ring, to measure his courage and virility against a similarly unprotected opponent. The sense of raw man-to-man combat in a wild setting in front of a motley crowd adds a dimension of carnival conviviality and exuberance to the event, a dimension effectively captured in the film version of Palahniuk's text.

My own experiment in this field was, however, motivated not so much by manly aspirations but happened more or less accidentally one drunken evening after a few pints with my friend and regular sparring partner, Alan. Al was a keen player in the Gaelic sport of hurling, a speciality of the town of Kilkenny from which he hailed, and one in which he had shown great promise in his youth. His face was marked by almost imperceptible scars that bore witness to the hits in the face he had taken in his teenage years. Having just failed to make his mark nationally in hurling, Al seems to have decided, while pursuing his additional talents as artist and philosopher, to concentrate on building his body, which, by the time I encountered him on a more or less daily basis in the College gym, was already in an enviable state of development. In mid-winter Al would still wander around College in a short-sleeved sports shirt, his well-muscled biceps glowing white in the grey light. At that time, I was having trouble trying to get the better of another young heavyweight called Ruari I was teaching to box and with whom I was regularly sparring. I would periodically complain to Al of the frequent and painful body blows Ruari would administer but I would receive by way of sympathy no more than a delighted chuckle and the admonition, 'You must learn to cover up, man!'

Eventually Al was persuaded to join in the boxing which he entered into with the same commitment and flair that he showed in his other sport. Sometimes we would train in the garden early on a Saturday morning, following the set-to with breakfast and a few beers. Al was one of the few boxers I've fought to give me a bleeding nose, but also confidence, in that I sometimes landed something good in return (though he would always say he let me hit him). It was one evening in the summer after a few pints that, back at my house, while mulling over boxing moves and comparing our respective fighting style, we began spontaneously to throw friendly punches at each other. The set-to imperceptibly became more serious and at one stage we were going hammer and tongs on the hearthrug until I decided regretfully, but no doubt wisely, to call a halt. Being well tanked up meant that the bare-knuckle blows we exchanged did not really hurt and it was only the following morning that with some dismay I realised I had a hefty bruise on my right bicep, and a cut lip. The worst of the set-to was thus, as is usually the case in these circumstances, the Inconvenience, not of the Bleeding Nose, but of having to explain to family and friends how I had come by the cuts and bruises. It was also embarrassing for Al to see the next day marked on my body the result of his previous night's handiwork, but, since between sparring partners exchanges of blows are part of the game, he and I remain the best of friends.

10. Boxing in the Snow

Luke was the keenest boxer I ever encountered. He was also one of the hardest hitters. He, as much as anyone I met in the ring, answered to the description of punching well above his weight.

He was a mere supermiddleweight in build but he put an energy and commitment into his punches that was out of all proportion to his stature. After a certain point, I had to give up sparring in the same ring as he: I could take the apple-sized bruises he imprinted on my right bicep when narrowly missing my chin with a right cross, or even the occasional sickening punch above the kidney. But when his right hook connected with the left side of my head, there were times when I thought I'd emerge from the ring either deaf in one ear or with my left-hand eyesight seriously impaired. At other times a cracking blow to the head would result in a glimpse of stars accompanied by a sudden splitting head-ache, mercifully short-lived, but an indication that something in the brain was being badly scrambled.

However, Luke was always so keen to get in the ring for a scrap of some kind that I sometimes foolishly relented and consented to a (so-called) shadow-spar or light move around. As he was often abroad, he would often reactivate our intermittent friendship by initiating a set-to within hours of his return to Dublin. One very cold winter, when it was reported that the sweat on the boxers training in Arbor Hill Boxing Club froze as soon as they stopped moving, and the ringside sponges were solid with ice, Luke was arriving back from the Lebanon where he was writing a book. Although he had located a boxing club in a distant suburb of that city and encountered sparring partners suitably challenging, he was keen to lace on the gloves as soon as he was home. So I found myself obliged to respond to his plaintive text message saying, 'Is there any boxing going on?' The boxing gym being closed (it was just before Christmas), I jokingly suggested a move-around in my snow-filled back garden, in the spot designated in finer weather for outdoor sparring. The offer was taken up seriously, so that evening two tall and wiry figures stripped down to boxing shorts and T-shirts could just about be made out jabbing and ducking in the cold air, the heat of their bodies creating a halo of condensation as they slid over the compacted snow of the improvised ring. The slipperiness of the ground and the occasional icy drip from an overhanging tree provided additional hazards to the encounter, but, given the conditions, the only stars that were seen were those twinkling in the wintry sky, not those anticipated on the receipt of a sharp blow to the head. The inconclusive outcome of the fight was celebrated with a hot whiskey and a brisk rub-down in front of a blazing fire. Such are the rewards of boxing in the snow.

11. Mixed Martial Arts in a Pine Wood

The regulation and control to which boxing has been submitted over the last century has led in the last two decades to a resurgence of interest in more basic forms of man-to-man or hand-to-hand combat. This has manifested itself not only in the increasing popularity of Far-Eastern martial arts but also in the various ways these have been adapted or adulterated in the West in the form of Cage Fighting, Mixed Martial Arts and Full Contact Fighting. The appeal of these sports lies in both the no-holds-barred approach and the variability of moves and hits that can be explored, plus the intense visceral excitement always generated when two male bodies come into violent contact with each other. Mixed martial arts in this way provide not only a range of sometimes unanticipated experiences for participants but also, from an artistic perspective, the possibility of exploring new ways of representing the human body.

My friend Fergus, as a wrestler and MMA enthusiast as well as a fine draughtsman and innovative performance artist, is ideally placed to explore both aspects of these sports' appeal and, in addition, the ways the two perspectives can enrich each other. Fergus is also a keen cyclist so one summer's day I suggested I take him to visit a Traveler's boxing ring that had been erected in a remote corner of the foothills of the Wicklow Mountains, near the Lead Mines above Kilternan. After a fairly grueling climb up some steep laneways – my nose was so close to the incline being negotiated that it would have served as a useful brake had a sudden halt been required – we reached the pine forest in which the gypsy ring was concealed. The bikes had to be hidden in a thicket before we clambered up the steep wooded incline to find the rustic boxing ring. To my initial disappointment, the ring, though still there, had lost its canvas and its floor so what we were confronted with was a kind of roped-in cage with a muddy and steeply sloping base formed by the side of the hill.

We nevertheless managed to worm our way through the web of enclosed ropes and find ourselves facing each other in the charmed cube. Almost without discussion we found ourselves with a grin peeling off our jackets and shirts and beginning to square up in a boxing posture that soon evolved into an interesting scrap. Fergus's training in MMA and my movements as a conventional boxer evolved into a complicated tussle in which his unprotected belly became the target of my standard boxing blows to the body while the extraordinary agility and speed of his arms and legs had me at times in very awkward positions: I was not used to being dumped on the ground so easily and so often, so when after a few minutes of struggle we called a halt to the proceedings, we were both as smeared with mud and sweat as any native Indian after combat in the wild.

Duly elated, we threw our kit back on and jogged back to the bikes where a supply of chocolate and fruit were a welcome replenishment to the body after its unexpected exertions. Since then, we have agreed to try to locate other sites of possible interesting pugilistic interaction, but I doubt we will find another offering as much raw wildness and visceral poetry as the gypsy ring in the pine wood.

12. White-Collar Boxing in Dublin Hotels

White-collar fighting, though only a middle-aged man's version of amateur boxing, embraces some of the showier aspects of professional boxing: outlandish trunks and dressing gowns, absurd fight sobriquets, loud introductory music and glamorous fight settings. Irish white-collar boxing is no exception to this rule, the fight venues usually being hotel restaurants or places set up for use as such. So Jury's Hotel, the City West and the Mansion House have over the last decade been the showcase of Irish white-collar boxing. Competing in such settings is proportionately more nerve-racking as the noise, the distance of the ring from the changing area, the extravagant entry of some of the fighters (on one occasion, a boxer entered astride his heavy motorbike) all challenge the nervous fighter attempting to concentrate on his game plan and keep his nerves under control. The boxer is scarcely reassured by the partisan applause of the audience, largely made up of tables more motivated to support individual fighters than to appreciate the merits and skills of the boxing in general. The supporters are, furthermore, naturally as interested in enjoying their expensive dinners as admiring the travails of the faceless middle-aged boxers sweating it out in front of them.

But the most unsettling aspect of white-collar boxing is one that besets the sport in general – that of waiting. Boxers turn up hours before the proceedings commence to have their medical check-over, get changed, make their ceremonial entrance as a group before retiring to the changing room to await their slot in the programme. Very often this can mean hanging about for several hours in an improvised changing area were the forlorn fighter is left hungry, anxious and cold, trying to hang onto his gear and his motivation among the comings and goings of the other boxers. By the time a fighter's name is announced, his main concern is to get the bout over and to go back home for a bath and rest.

However, on stepping into the ring, the deity presiding over Boxing works his magic, and the fighter is transformed into an eager and excited combatant, ready to go out and give his all to the contest. While the white-collar fights I lost disappear into a blur of fatigue and adrenaline, the ones I won were experienced in slower motion, the shots landed being more dispassionately noted, the feints and parries more accurately measured and the outcome more a foregone conclusion. Whatever the verdict, however, the aftermath of the white-collar bout, like most fights, offers its momentary high as the tension and adrenaline that unify and synergize mind and body are released in a way that it seems only boxing can do.

III Schoolboy Rites of Passage

1. Juvenile Priapism

I must have been about seven, the age when children of either sex commonly disappear in small groups into a coal hole or garden shed where, in the sooty privacy of the one or the pine-scented warmth of the other, knickers and underpants would be dropped and the sexual parts of the participants shamelessly bared. But the initial reaction to this mutual exposure was not so much sexual arousal as unstoppable and infectious laughter, so that when the young partners later emerged from their den of precocious iniquity they were flushed less with sexual excitement than with a kind of communal jubilance and hilarity – a function as much of their newfound awareness of the supposed nighttime activities of their parents as an imitation of it.

As with many experiences of childhood, related areas of knowledge – sexual, emotional, environmental – could develop for a while quite separately from each other, so that, for example, laughter or excitement could be enjoyed independently of a certain perception of incongruity or the burgeoning of the libido. So my first remembered experience of an erection was stimulated not by the presence of another partly naked body but by the action of relieving myself in the lavatory one bright morning before heading off on a fishing outing. For some reason, possibly associated with the hunting expedition I was about to set out on, I decided, instead of simply lifting the leg of my brown corduroy shorts in the boyish way to allow my penis to direct its flow into the lavatory basin, to slowly and methodically unbutton the flies of my trousers, separating the tails of my shirt so that my cock could emerge from my underpants before pissing directly into the toilet bowl. When the operation was complete and I manoeuvred my organ back beneath my clothing, I found to my surprise and pleasure that it was tumescent and remained hard for some time after I quitted the bathroom, picked up my fishing tackle and headed out to meet the other boys before descending to the stream.

In the increasing warmth of that morning as I sat in my shirtsleeves on the river bank casting the primitive bamboo rod and waited for the bobbing of the float that signalled a bite, I discovered that I was able periodically to summon at will the satisfying swelling in my trousers. And when after a while something silvery and insistent emerged wriggling from the water at the end of the line attached to my rod, my ejaculation of surprise and pleasure was expressed in a shout of triumph to the other boys.

2. Physical Jerks

It is notoriously difficult for a man to remember his first ejaculation. He thinks it must have been earlier than he remembers while his first definite recollection of the event may be one that at the time he might prefer not to recount to fellow males as he feels it may do him little credit. Masturbation, though everyone knows it is widespread and long-standing among men of any age, was until quite recently a taboo subject, so that the many forms and times in which it was practiced remained in my youth nearly as uncharted a territory as male sexuality in general before the Kinsey report of over half a century ago.

My earliest masturbatory fantasies, dating back to that late childhood/early pubescent period (between the ages of nine and eleven), have as much to do with managing the change from a boyish to a manly body – the regretted but necessary need to give over teddy bear and toys for chest-expanders or boxing gloves – as with confrontation with sex, or even just another's sexual potential. So that my first fully conscious remembrance of an ejaculation (setting aside those wet dreams, the evidence of which could only be confirmed by laundry maids, washerwomen or an overly vigilant mother) was connected with physical training at school. PT and circuit training were a discipline to which the pubescent boy's relatively unformed body was subjected with the aim of developing strength and muscle, grace and speed of movement and a sense of physical and mental confidence. Stripped naked except for gym shoes and a pair of thin white cotton shorts, schoolboys were regularly submitted to circuit routines, including jumping on and off low benches, medicine-ball throwing and catching, burpees, press-ups, crunches, gate-vaulting, and other exercises designed to strengthen the body's core as well as the limbs, increase stamina and resilience and generally to instill a sense of physical power and potential.

It was the curiously-named burpee exercise that I found most disturbing: it involved squatting on the floor with arms at full length and then repeatedly kicking out the legs backwards from a crouch to a fully extended position, usually at a rate of twelve to twenty repetitions. The similarity of this exercise to that of the sexual act had escaped me until one occasion when I doing this routine at the end of a circuit in which I was falling behind the other boys; wishing at all costs to avoid being the last to complete the round (the reward for which was an extra circuit), I put on a spurt which had the surprising and embarrassing effect of sudden and intense sexual arousal, a tingling in my testicles that signaled imminent ejaculation. I somehow managed to finish the routine without jerking off and quickly enough to avoid the imposition of an extra circuit which went to another boy who had fumbled with the medicine ball and lost his pace and rhythm.

When at home and in the privacy of the bathroom later that night I decided to do the burpee experiment again and see to what extent it could be used as a means of reproducing the sexual act. So stripped naked, I squatted on the floor between the lavatory and the basin, and started the routine: however, to my initial disappointment, my swift and rhythmic execution of the exercise failed to bring about the sexual arousal that had so startled and embarrassed me in the gym earlier that day. However, once I was well above the twenty or so jerks that were the usual measure of the routine, and increasing the pace as far as my now sweating body would allow, I felt the warning tingle in the balls and was soon reaching that point of indescribable ecstasy at which the combined energies of the body seem to explode in a fireball of visceral pleasure. The hot sperm came pumping from my cock, staining the bath mat and exuding the heady odour of male potency that it had been the aim of the experiment for me to prove to myself. So that when, after showering, I stepped out of the bathroom in a clean white shirt and with freshly slicked hair, as if I had just exited the school gym after a grueling but satisfying hour of physical training, I felt I had now understood what was at stake in the onset of male sexuality.

3.   Back seat Snogging

As a boy, sitting upstairs on the back seat of the bus home from school with the girls was an initiation into sexual pleasure. It involved a deliberate choice: not to stay downstairs with the bespectacled lad and get the maths prep done on the way home; not to go upstairs to the front where the young smoking fraternity, ties and school blazers doffed, were casually rolling cigarettes and counting the puffs before the bus conductor clambered up threatening to report them. Promises of hidings by fathers or headmasters were laughed off and, in any case, the mirror at the top of the bus stairs that enabled the conductor to keep an eye on the stairwell also served as a warning to the smokers, who always had a boy posted on look-out. Boys and girls indulging in activity on the upstairs back seat also had to beware of this tell-tale glass, though the mischief of the tobacco rollers up front were usually a sufficient decoy for the fumblings going on at the rear.

The backseat activity, with loosened tie and lowered stockings, involved much touch and grope, though the boys seemed keener to let their hands explore the mysteries beneath the summer frocks than did those of the girls the priapic bulging of grey shorts. Snogging was the main focus, the blissful relapse into the saliva-ed haven of the other's mouth, with all its accompanying sensuous and sexual stirrings, leading to a state of quasi oblivion that was often rudely disturbed by the bus's sudden slowing at the approach of the home bus-stop. The possessor of the aroused penis had quickly to fix his belt and grab his satchel and school-cap before sliding down the stairs at the last moment, the erection still swelling his trousers impeding his jump-off as the bus jerked to a stand-still.

4.   First Love in the Lane

A young man's first taste of sex is seldom the complete, unmitigated pleasure that he imagines it should be. Mine was around the age of eighteen and involved a cousin from Canada who was staying with her mother on a visit to my family home in a remoter part of Norfolk. I was as hopelessly drawn by the soft dark hair and sensuous body of Stephanie as by her bright-eyed playfulness and lack of inhibition. I was surprised how suddenly I preferred lolling about without jacket or tie and would in the morning dawdle in only trousers and singlet on the way back from the bathroom after shaving. I was similarly alert to my cousin's appearance, in particular in the bright green dress that seemed, while contrasting with her skin, to harmonize so well with the verdure of the summer hedgerows. We would flirt and cuddle unselfconsciously in front of the family group who seemed to take a benign view of our seemingly harmless friendship.

One warm evening, however, when as usual we set out along the narrow country road leading to our house to indulge in the snogging that had become the habitual climax of our days together, my arousal and her excitement reached a point at which a fumbling attempt at intercourse was enacted. Unfortunately at precisely that moment, a car passed along the lane on whose verge we were entwined. The car can only have been that of a visitor to our house as it was the lane's only possible destination. As we feared, therefore, the act intercepted by the car's headlights would already have been recounted to the family group by the unwitting visitor, and the return of the subsequent young lovers greeted with anything but approbation.

However, the irritation of my mother was less a function of the natural fulfillment of her son's teenage urges than of the memory, unbeknownst to me, of her jealousy as a young woman of Stephanie's mother Jane. I later learned that my grandmother had taken Jane as a young teenager into her family when her own mother left her father (my granny's brother) for another man. My mother, a single child, had somewhat resented the presence of the slightly older cousin, not least since her romantic experiments seemed to be tolerated more freely than her own. So to see her cousin's daughter freely and precociously engaging sexually with her son perhaps reignited her jealousy, causing an irritation that was misdirected towards the young lovers.

The upshot of this was that my feeling of triumph and fulfillment at a successful first enactment of sex with a woman was dampened both by the anxiety and embarrassment of its immediately being witnessed, and by the disquiet of my mother, the causes of which I was then oblivious, but for which, as her eldest son, I felt in some way responsible. However, the event was soon forgotten, as was the holiday romance which, despite its unplanned moment of climax, had no further repercussions; it was soon just a happy memory. However, the pure, untrammelled joy that it might have vouchsafed was dimmed forever by the thin cloud of guilt that, as I was to learn, rarely fails to overshadow even the acutest pleasure.

5.   Schoolboy Uniform

A major feature of the move from primary to secondary school within the British state system was the shift from freedom of dress to a strict adoption of uniform. (This change was initiated at a traumatically earlier date for preparatory – or 'prep' – school boys, at the age of seven or eight, whereby infants who had barely learned to tie their shoelaces had also to master the art of tying ties and to remember to wear – on pain of punishment – the regulation school cap.) It marked the shift from the relative freedom of young childhood to the more disciplined environment of the grown-up world, almost a parody enactment, for boys in particular, of the military, business or professional world into which their parents mostly hoped they would evolve.

The uniform was fairly standard across the British Isles from the 1930s to the 1970s (and beyond): it consisted of grey (or less usually white) shirt, grey shorts and socks; black shoes; there was the obligatory School blazer (usually black or navy blue) and the School cap and tie, though the wearing of the cap seems to have died out after the late 1960s. Underwear was regulation white underpants (later boxer shorts) and vests.

The predominance of grey – the dullest and most neutral of hues – as the uniform colour was a further sign of the suppression of individual fantasy as expressed in bright or outlandish clothing and a premonition of the subdued tones –

black, navy blue, khaki, blue or brown – that became standard for adult males in the post-war period before the 1960s. The one bright note was provided by the school tie, which usually involved stripes of crimson, green or gold, and the school badge, worn on the cap and the breast pocket of the blazer. These signs of collegial allegiance would later be valued by the grown-up schoolboy as they constituted marks of his passage and were at the same time tokens of recognition to other males of a shared educational background.

A number of variations of school uniform, some permitted according to the standard regulations, others instigated to bend the rules, were adopted, the choice increasing as the boy grew more senior. After the age of fourteen or fifteen boys were allowed to swap shorts for trousers and after the age of sixteen were sometimes allowed to relax slightly the adjustment of their clothes: the blazer need only be fastened by one rather than three buttons; the tie removed during the summer term. At various stages during the fashion-conscious 1960s, unofficial innovations were sometimes tolerated: more or less pointed shoes and shirts with button-down collars. Ties could be slightly loosened, the top shirt-button undone, and shirtsleeves rolled (up to the biceps in the early 1960s, just above the wrist later in the decade). The prestige or standing of the individual schoolboy could often be judged by the daring he showed in modifying his apparel to stylish effect while managing to stay – just – within the general school regulations. Hairstyles were similar standardized as far as possible (the military 'short back and sides' prevailed well into the sixties) with some headmasters insisting on hairstyles with partings; a lavish application of haircream in the fifties and early sixties was suddenly abandoned from the mid-1960s when the male pop band established a new norm with longer, more freely flowing hair.

Official variations in dress were usually restricted to the addition to the top pocket of the blazer of school colours in medal-like stripes (awarded for proficiency in sports or house matches) while prefects' and house captains' rank was marked by a varying number of bands of gold braid affixed military-style round the cuffs of their jackets.

The arrival of the new uniform came as a surprise, pleasant or unpleasant as the case may be, not least in that it constituted a complete kit of clothes. Perfectly pressed grey shirts came wrapped in cellophane and had to be released from pins and cardboard stiffeners before they could be worn; the smell of fresh cotton was a harbinger of the approaching new school year with all that it might bring in terms of dread or excitement. New shoes and sports gear offered a different range of olfactory sensations ranging from new leather (satchels, shoes, football boots, boxing gloves) to wood and catgut (cricket bats, tennis rackets), while the heavy drill of rugby shorts and cricket flannels had a special fragrance. All garments – uniform or sports – had nametapes sewn onto them and thus identified themselves as the sole property of their wearers. In this way the boy's identity became attached to his uniform.

This convention could have tiresome consequences. I remember the teasing I suffered and the embarrassment I felt when the nametapes on my sports gear were identified in the changing room before or after gym or a match. My mother had ordered that the full panoply of my initials – D. H. T. – precede my surname on the tapes on all my gear, even down to my rugby socks, so that when quizzed by other boys as to what the initials stood for, I had to admit to DAVID HENRY TUDOR, a suite of names the pronouncement of which resulted in howls of derision and, subsequently, endless ragging about qualities I may or may not have shared with the Tudor monarch with whom my name ineluctably identified me. In this way, a seemingly trivial detail in schoolboy accoutrements could, if identified from an outside or otherwise unsympathetic perspective, unlock a Pandora's box of unsuspected associations that he had to take on board and defend, awakening in him the realisation that, like life, his story was not as simple as it seemed, but had attached to it all kinds of historical or other associations that, though not of his choosing, might nevertheless be imputed to him.

6. Six of the Best

I remember as a boy reading with surprise in a book I got as a school prize – it was one of C. S. Forester's famous Hornblower books (*Lieutenant Hornblower* I think) – that boys were frequently beaten without cause since 'contact with injustice in a world that was essentially unjust was part of everyone's education'. Further, that 'grown men smiled to each other when boys were beaten, agreeing that it did all parties good; boys had been beaten since history began, and it would be a bad day for the world if ever, inconceivably, boys should cease to be beaten'. Some years later I learnt about the initiation rites to which many indigenous tribes submitted boys at puberty to ensure their safe passage to manhood – sometimes involving such apparently brutal treatment as the knocking out of a tooth (as in Aboriginal Australia), the filing down of top front teeth (as in Indonesia), beating and banishment to the wilderness (in various African tribes). In the light of this it occurred to me that the old British way with rites of masculine passage – whether in the armed services or in boarding school, where boys were regularly caned by prefects and schoolmasters – was merely a latter-day continuation of a primeval practice.

So as George Orwell, Roald Dahl and other writers have recorded, six of the best was, until caning was banned in most British boys' schools from the early 1970s, part of the rite of passage from boyhood to manhood, like military training in the Combined Cadet Force or the obligation to board away from home. Of course, within the school context, beatings were delivered principally as punishment for breaking rules; they were not consciously recognised as part of a ritual of deeper significance. Delivered by a senior boy or house-captain, as well as by house-master or school head, a caning was the promptest, most rapid and efficient way of punishing misdemeanours of a seriousness ranging from forgetting to wear the uniform cap while out of the school grounds to cheating in examinations.

Senior boys – perhaps unconsciously imitating the zeal of their so-called primitive forbears – tended to show the most severity in the delivery of their punishment, realizing that the greater the pain they inflicted on their hapless victims the higher would be their prestige within the schoolboy community, not to mention their reputation as effective disciplinarians. Housemasters, whose authority was well established, tended on the whole to be more perfunctory in their application of the usual quota of strokes: the interview in the comfortable, club-like office with its leather armchair and mahogany desk, the brisk announcement of the punishment to be inflicted, followed swiftly by its execution, prior to which the hapless boy had scarcely time to remove his jacket and adopt the bending posture requisite for the impending beating. After the six strokes, the boy was promptly dismissed from the study and left to deal as best he could with the pain searing his posterior.

Headmasters, depending on their personality, permitted themselves a wider variety of caning styles as well as a larger number of strokes using a rattan or bamboo cane, applied either in a chaotic shower or carefully configured into a geometrical pattern on the (sometimes) bared posterior. Birchings were the most extreme form of discipline, the dozen or so strokes of which created a tangle of welts and bruises that it took at least a week for the bottom to recover from. The worst of the birching was that the miscreant boy's father would at the end of term be billed for the broom-like birch rod that was, after one use, normally discarded. This charge had the disadvantage to the boy of his parent being alerted to the punishment he had received, which could lead on his return home to further painful consequences. In this way – in what we would today refer to as a double whammy – the father paid twice over in cash for the rite of passage of the son who himself sometimes paid twice over in the beatings he suffered in vouchsafing it. In such a way was the pre-1970 British schoolboy doubly prepared for the injustices of the world.

7.   The Visit to the Barber

A trip to the barber was as a good a way of spoiling Saturday morning as any other in schoolboy memory. The hair was just beginning to grow thick enough over the neck to preclude the need of a scarf in winter, when the monthly injunction from my father, an RAF officer, over breakfast to get a haircut had dutifully to be obeyed, and the neck and sides of the head mercilessly exposed once more to the elements. The 'short back and sides cut' was administered with uncompromising rigour by the military-station barber to whom I was told to go.

First there was the wait in the cramped barber's shop, the fake leather couch encumbered with newspapers, mostly open at the sports pages – cricket, soccer and boxing seemed to be the barber and his clients' main interests – or at those revealing the scandalous bodies and lives of minor starlets or actresses. 'The hottest thing in Las Vegas, that's what they're calling me now' was a headline from *The Daily Mirror* from around 1959 that stuck in my memory; it was the caption to an article by Diana Dors who was the then British answer to Jane Mansfield. Who 'they' were was never entirely clear to me, but there seemed at the time to be little doubt of their judgement in relation to that parody of British sexuality that was the blond bombshell from Berkshire. But the paper also offered other fantasy images, in particular the body-building ads that promised a rapid conversion of the physique from that of the 'seven-stone weakling' to the magnificently muscular Hercules, who, in the form of Charles Atlas, displayed his rippling abs and leopardskin swimming trunks as an impossibly desirable aim for the puny schoolboy.

The walls of the barber's shop were enlivened by the usual photos of sportsmen, in particular cricketers, footballers and boxers, whose shiny, usually black hair, was an unacknowledged tribute to the heavy application of the oil that was advertised in the posters and fliers that decorated those same walls. Indeed the adverts for Brylcreem, with their doggerel catch phrases 'Brylcreem, a little dab will do ya/Boys watch out, the girls will all pursue ya', or 'Brylcreem, the perfect hairdressing', or, most arresting, 'A man *needs* Brylcreem', were a permanent feature of the space and a prelude to that dreaded moment when a liberal dose would be applied to the schoolboy head. For the 1950s schoolboy was never consulted about the arrangement of his hair: the back and sides of his head were uncompromisingly shaved, a side parting was defined, the longer hair on one side was swept back in a heavily greased quiff. It would have been as inconceivable for the boy to decline the hair cream as it would for adult male customers to forgo the option of 'A little something extra for the weekend', a phrase whose meaning only became clear to me several years later after repeated observation of the furtive transaction that was negotiated as the newly shorn adult customer paid his bill.

In the days that followed, the oiled quiff got flattened by the schoolboy cap whose inside rim got greasy, and the blazer collar had to be turned up, when safely out of school limits, to protect the exposed neck. The comb as well as the hairbrush became a necessary part of the morning toilet and having to wash the hair with shampoo was an ordeal almost as unpleasant as that of the trip to the barber itself. Despite periodic showering, it took several days for the Brylcreem to wash out and several weeks for the hair to grow back again to a comfortable length before the cycle had to be repeated all over again.

8. The Price of a First Smoke

The initiation to smoking was a standard part of early adolescence for most boys. It was taken as a sign of approaching manhood: some lads even went to the extent of yellowing their cigarette finger with carrot juice to give the impression of the nicotine stains that were the mark of a hardened addict; and even at the risk of a beating (smoking at school was strictly prohibited), they liked to exhibit their shirt pocket bulging with the rectangular cigarette packet it contained and did not bother to hide the rattle of the matchbox in their trousers.

In my case, the first cigarette was not entirely pleasurable despite it being shared with my best schoolfriend, David Woods, who had a knack of making the smallest of misdemeanours a furtive adventure. Woodsie's air of quiet insolence as much as his mischievousness resulted in his being the boy who managed to get himself caned more frequently than any other in his year at school, but he always shrugged off the beatings with the surprising assertion that 'It's good to suffer a bit of pain'.

One night he asked me round to his house, ostensibly to show me his new boxing gloves, but mainly to share an illicit smoke. When up in his bedroom, he fished the packet of cigarettes from where they were hidden up the chimney of the small bedroom fireplace. Under the cover of the autumn dark, the fag was lit and shared as we stood at the open window. In his efforts to make me properly inhale I suffered a fit of coughing that I tried unsuccessfully to suppress, but unfortunately not before Woodsie's father, an RAF sergeant, came bounding upstairs to see what the matter was. Quick as a flash the lighted cigarette was flicked through the open window, but the tell-tale smell of smoke was enough to betray the cause of my coughing fit.

Promptly sent packing, I was scarcely halfway down the garden path when I heard through the still open bedroom window the fearsome crack of Woodsie's Dad's leather belt resounding on my hapless mate's backside. I lived in dread over the next few days of the misdeed being reported to my father, but the Woods were decent enough not to inform on me, and David never bore me a grudge for earning him an extra bit of pain through my inability to inhale.

9.   First Flicks

The cinema began for me to exert its attraction at about the same time as television – at the approach of adolescence at the end of the 1950s. Television was black and white at that stage and the programmes I watched were mainly American serial westerns (*Bronco*, *Laramee*) or sports matches (especially amateur boxing). This was the moment also when pop music, in particular as channelled through Radio Luxembourg, became an irresistible source of discovery and excitement. The first adult movie I remember seeing – *The Dambusters* – was in the cinema on the RAF base in North Yorkshire where my father was posted. It was a memorable event not only because it was one of the rare occasions when my dad took me to see or do anything, but also because it was an evening showing, and not a matinée as I had been used to until then. It meant leaving the house in the dark and also, on the insistence of my dad, smartly dressed in my school uniform with my hair freshly cut and oiled so that I would appear presentable among the officers and airmen who would be watching the film.

The small cinema was crammed, mostly with servicemen in uniform, so I found myself occupying a seat in a sloping sea of RAF blue. The film was preceded by the playing of the national anthem, during which the entire audience stood, myself included, though only after a sharp nudge from my father. In those days, most adults smoked, particularly in their leisure time, so very soon a pall of tobacco fumes hung overhead, and before long my eyes, unused to the smoky assault, were smarting.

The Dambusters is not really a film suitable for the young: much of the earlier part is devoted to dialogue and discussion as the ingeniously lethal devices invented by Barnes Wallace are developed and tested. It is only during the final action stage that an average boy's attention would be roused from boredom and incomprehension as the risky bombing sorties to the Eder and Möhne dams got underway. The drone of the Lancaster bombers, the clipped commentary of the pilots and crew, the tension as the aircraft approached their difficult and heavily armed targets, built up to an almost intolerable crescendo of excitement, which was released only as the bombs were dropped, aircraft were shot down or exploded in midair, the dams were pierced by the bouncing bombs and, most memorable of all, the rushing waves of water released from the reservoirs in one short sequence engulfed a car attempting to speed away from the catastrophe.

The poignant dirge of the Dambusters' March was still ringing in my ears as with bleary eyes and tie awry I exited the cinema among the jostling and tobacco-smelling servicemen. My father offered little in the way of commentary on the film, but the dark night outside the cinema building seemed to have a depth to it I had never noticed before, one pregnant with terrors and possibilities that the cinema, as I had now discovered, was uniquely apt at intimating.

10. Combined Cadet Force

The Combined Cadet Force or CCF was one of the first surprises
to strike the grammar- or private-school boy on his promotion
to secondary-level education. Incorporated into the boy's school
curriculum on the phasing out in Britain in the mid-1950s of
the National Service scheme, the CCF was conceived to give
boys as they became young men the discipline, knowledge and
fitness associated with the armed services and instil in them an
ethos of loyalty and duty to their country. So on Mondays boys
turned up for school in army uniform with, in later years, the
option of changing to RAF or Naval service, according to their
preference – or, more likely, that of their father.

The first thing one had to learn was to show up promptly for
parade on Mondays in impeccable kit. This involved devoting
the best part of the preceding Sunday to applying a flaky khaki
substance called blanco to the webbing belt worn as part of the
army battledress; to polishing the brass buckle and fastener on
the trouser belt, ensuring that no Brasso dripped onto and thus
blackened the webbing; to bringing the heavy black army boots
to the correct level of shine. Getting the blanco to the right
slightly flaky consistency and the correct shade of khaki was a
fine art, as also was ironing a crease into the heavy drill combat
trousers. The thick and ticklish flannel army shirt had to be
properly tucked in and the khaki tie immaculately pressed.
Meanwhile, the black beret had to be placed at exactly the right
angle on the freshly Brylcreemed head, the hair of which had
to be cut so short at the back and sides that it was scarcely
visible. The beret could only be removed, folded and placed in
the epaulette of the left shoulder of the battle-dress or of the
shirt when the cadet was not marching or on the parade ground
but involved in a less regimented military task, such as oiling his
rifle or pouring over an ordnance survey map. In the summer,
'shirtsleeve order' was specified, which meant that, for the

greater comfort of the cadets, ties and battle-dress jacket could be removed, shirt collar unbuttoned and shirtsleeves rolled up to the requisite level above the elbow. The inspecting Sergeant Major would immediately identify any fault in uniform presentation, the punishment for which would be extra drill at the double or the requirement to run repeated circuits of the parade ground with a rifle held over the head.

Much of the training was repetitive: lots of rifle routines – presenting and shouldering arms; standing to attention and at ease; this could be very trying, especially on hot summer days, when to prevent the risk of passing out, cadets were instructed periodically to flex the muscles in their knees. And there was lots of marching. The latter was strangely enjoyable as the individual cadet became at one with a corps of young men moving in step and according to the monotonous but haunting rhythm drummed out by the accompanying army band or 'Corps of Drums'. Longer marches sometimes led the squad out of the school yard onto country roads where, particularly in summer and when in shirtsleeve order, the fresh air, warm sun and the rhythm of regimented movement gave rise to a strange sense of well-being.

Much time was also spent on maintaining the army rifle each cadet was issued with and getting plenty of shooting practice in the rifle range that was sited in a corner of the school playing field. The satisfaction of seeing returned to the rifleman the small cardboard targets with bullet marks near the bull's-eye was one of the more agreeable aspects of this activity, preferable to the obligation to complete a gruelling assault course that had been rigged up in a dell at another corner of the field: the requirement to swing across gullies, clamber up rope ladders, step across wooden platforms fully kitted with rifle and haversack was a testing discipline. For me the biggest trial was mastering a tendency to vertigo which meant always looking up rather than down when negotiating manoeuvres at any height.

On days when the weather was too wet to train outside, there were prolonged sessions in the gym, including circuit training, vaulting, rope-climbing and any other activity that resembled something done on an assault course. Boxing also figured prominently within the physical training programme, with inter-platoon bouts being periodically organised to maintain, so we were told, the competitive spirit and to keep us on our mettle. The more academic side of the CCF programme included map-reading, exercises in logistics (food, shelter, transport) and some military strategy. Occasionally, former members of the armed forces would be invited to lecture to us on their war experiences or on other challenges relating to the military life, the most entertaining of which involved the recounting of the god-awful cock-ups that bedevil even the best-trained army. These speakers would invariably turn up in uniform, confirming the suspicion that, whatever their age, men as well as boys like dressing up and playing at soldiers.

11. Military Camp

In the second year of the school I went to in the early 1960s, the one day a week of soldiering in the CCF was diversified in that each boy was offered the choice of either staying in the army or opting for the Navy or the RAF. Since I was the son of an RAF officer, recently retired from the forces, the choice of the latter was for me automatic, especially as it offered the possibility of spending week-long summer camps on an RAF base. Having spent the first decade of my life as an RAF kid, feelings of nostalgia for the smartly and logically regimented spaces of the typical air-force base were still strong, as was the potential for adventure that the aerodrome offered with its air-raid shelters, pill-boxes, rifle ranges and abandoned pre-war cars.

I was happy to swap the uncomfortable army battle-dress

with its webbing belt and brass buckles for the smarter and more relaxed RAF uniform which comprised standard black shoes instead of boots and a more comfortable light cotton shirt, although the latter did bring with it the novel inconvenience – especially when flying – of a starched and separate collar. Contriving to fit the latter to the shirt with a collar stud and then insert and correctly fix the tie without smudging the RAF blue, was a delicate Monday-morning routine, and the nature of this neck-gear meant that in summer 'shirtsleeve order' did not include for RAF cadets the comfortable option of unbuttoning the shirt-collar and removing the tie.

The RAF in the 1960s seemed to the schoolboy the most exciting force in the country, with its supersonic interceptor fighters and its strangely configured jet V-bombers which carried the British nuclear deterrent in the form of atomic bombs. To see the delta-winged Avro Vulcan passing overhead like a giant flatiron in the sky was a memorable experience, as was that of glimpsing the Handley Page Victor bomber with its curious scimitar-shaped wings and its glazed and beak-like nose, or a formation of English Electric Lightnings that, from below, looked like a template of silver diamonds. How to equate the glamorous appearance of these machines with their destructive purpose, in other words, how to co-relate aesthetics and violence, was only beginning to dawn on the schoolboy consciousness. In any case, the business of how the fighters and bombers were to be kept serviced and ready for action was the chief aim of the RAF training cadets underwent, along with the logistics of management and running what was, in the case of each base, a self-contained and self-servicing system with its own fire brigade, medical centre, fuel depots, armaments stores, hangars, workshops and training facilities.

One week-long summer camp was spent at RAF Scampton in Lincolnshire, home of the famous 617 squadron, known as the 'Dambusters' since their exploits leading to the destruction

in 1943 of the Möhne and Eder water reservoirs that served
the Rhur industrial area in north-west Germany. Cadets were
allowed to crawl under the massive delta wings of the Vulcan
bombers that were currently operational from the station,
observe in these shapely but lethal machines the pods in which
the nuclear devices were housed, and climb into the cockpit
to be bemused by the myriad dials and instruments that pilot,
navigator and flight engineer managed during flight. The kit
worn by the bomber crew was a typically RAF mix of smart
casualness, the zip-up boiler suit with its leg pockets and light
belt, opening at the neck to reveal a neat collar and tie, the
ensemble set off by the peaked military cap.

But the RAF cadets training was not just a matter of
observation and briefing. At one camp, RAF Swanton Morley
in north Norfolk, cadets were taught how to glide and at
another how to fly a light training aircraft. Gliding was at first a
terrifying experience since the seeming miracle of the light but
engineless machine remaining airborne for many minutes on
end was difficult for the mind to grasp. However, with repeated
experience of rising on a current of warm air, soaring with the
convection and then using the wide wingspan of the aircraft
to make a slow circular descent, the brain eventually arrived
at an understanding of the physics involved, even if the body,
in particular the stomach, never got entirely used the queasy
feeling induced.

Flying was less of an intellectual conundrum but was also
a challenge to the physiology of the young body, in particular
the aftermath to an airborne manoeuvre known as looping the
loop. This as much as anything else marked a right of passage
to flying, one for which it was difficult for the budding pilot
to prepare since the effect of it was virtually indescribable.
On the day of initiation, the air cadet, more nervous than
usual, mounted the cockpit behind the pilot, strapped himself
tightly in with his seat belt and was borne aloft in the usual

way to a suitable altitude. The pilot then demonstrated a series of standard manoeuvres – banking to port and to starboard, making a shallow dive and an equally shallow ascent. He then announced the looping of the loop in which the aircraft would describe a 360-degree longitudinal turn. This involved a steep and sudden upward climb, a levelling out of the aircraft in an upside-down configuration, followed immediately by a steep dive and then a flattening out that would bring the aircraft back into its normal flight disposition. The sudden upward thrust jerked the air cadet's neck violently backward as the G-forces kicked into his young body; before he was able to recover from this he found himself upside down, feeling the contents of his battle-dress, following the force of gravity, slip from his pockets; then as the accelerating aircraft turned to level out, he felt his neck thrusting hard against the collar stud in his shirt, a sensation that was exacerbated by a sickening feeling in his belly followed by a retching movement in his throat. There was of course no question of easing the respiratory passage by unbuttoning the complicated separate collar of the RAF shirt. Besides, there was the more pressing need to avoid throwing up the contents of his stomach (a hearty RAF breakfast) that felt as if it had been left many metres behind the rest of his body in the latter part of the manoeuvre. It was only the eternity of several seconds after the aircraft had levelled out again that the cadet was able to control his throat and breathing, recovering sufficiently to voice a reply to the pilot's breezy enquiry 'Is everything ok back there?'

Other less demanding but still engaging activities included learning how to fold a parachute's silvery grey silk and mass of cords into what seemed an impossibly compact package, how the pins should be fitted to fighter pilots' ejector seats, or how instruments of measurement should be accurately calibrated. The philosophy of 'fail-safe' – the institution and observation of mechanisms that, in the failure of one system immediately activated another – was repeatedly inculcated into us, along with the idea of careful observation and attention in all routines and disciplines. Order and precision seemed to be the dominating qualities required of the potential RAF officer, along with the ethos of teamwork and the recognition that individual actors, whether fighter pilots or regimental commanders, were only the apex of a pyramid of coordinated technicians, an awe-inspiring ideal for the undisciplined schoolboys that we then mostly were.

12. Airforce Base Mischief

Royal Airforce bases to a boy in the late 1950s and '60s as well as being home wherever they happened to be situated in Great Britain, or even abroad, were also an adventure playground that provided endless possibilities for thrills and mischief. They were microcosms of the adult world, small cities with fire stations, hospitals, workshops, food stores and residential quarters, quite apart from the military and sports installations that airforce kids found particularly alluring. A source of additional fascination provided by the stations constructed before or during the Second World War was that they were camouflaged, which is to say that their walls and sometimes roofs were swathed in drab-colored paint to make them appear from the air indistinguishable from semi-natural landscape. This strange element added to the glamour of the military environment and provided a context for the kind of adventures that boys dreamt about or read about in comics.

A further dimension was the cosmopolitan makeup of the servicemen stationed on the air bases, a number of whom were American, Canadian or of other, sometimes exotic, extractions: on one base was stationed a Bentley-driving Siamese prince. This meant that Oldsmobiles and Studebakers (whose names seemed as long as the fins they sported) as well as German cars, imported by RAF servicemen who had been posted to Germany, were frequently to be seen exhibiting their chromium-plated bulk, as were many pre-war British models that were still running efficiently even into the early 1960s. I remember in particular my father's 1935 Riley Monaco, a vehicle exotic not only in its strange diamond-shaped windows, its fabric roof and wire wheels, but also because of the odour its dull red and black bodywork exuded (it was regularly polished with a strange but not unpleasant-smelling liquid) and the leather of the inflatable back seat. The discoloration of some of the window glass, that with age acquired an amber hue, meant that from within the passing landscape took on an unreal, extraterrestrial look. Some of the older cars would after a time be left abandoned in decommissioned sheds or garages scattered about the airforce base: these wrecks of Triumph Glorias or Morris Eights would become the sites of impromptu picnics, trysts with girlfriends or scenes of imagined car chases, activities that were usually hurried if not furtive since sooner or later a serviceman would appear on the scene to chase the miscreant motorists away.

Indeed, games of chase with servicemen were among the keenest pleasures of air-force base mischief. The rows of neatly aligned Nissan huts, many of which were divided into offices or workshops along a long central corridor, were a favourite site for dares: run along the corridor banging on every other door and out the other end without being caught. The price to pay for interception was the choice of being reported to the Group Captain of the base or being given a belting on the spot by the corporal or sergeant by whom the miscreant had been collared. An alternative and equally risky prank was to lurk outside the squash court while the men were playing, rush in and turn out the lights at the switch by the door, and then escape to hide beneath the stilts that raised the court above the ground and enjoy the shouts of the players' annoyance. Sooner or later one of us would be caught and suffer the fate meted out by the Nissan-hut sergeant.

Not least of the fascinations of air-force bases was their semi-underground nature. Because they had been liable to bombing during the Second World War, in addition to air-raid shelters, a number of the installation and amenities were either built underground or clothed in a heavy turf covering. I remember my amazement when one day seeking a hiding place in a chase I ran under a hummock of grass and collided with a punch-bag that was hanging from the roof of what turned out to be an underground gym. But it was the air-raid shelters and defensive pill-boxes themselves that were most alluring, not only because of the threat of danger still associated with them, but also because of what we learned of adult mischief that they had clearly also provided a setting for. So smashed bottles, crushed cigarette packets (occasionally providing the joy of a couple of crumpled but unsmoked Woodbines), used condoms, a stray item of underwear – nickers or underpants – evoked scenarios that simultaneously appalled and fascinated us, mixed pleasures enhanced by the air-raid shelter's smell of urine, stale beer and damp. In this respect, air-raid shelters supplied a paradigm of the mischievous possibilities of the air-force base in general in that they provided a stage on which the young could act out in their own way what they perceived to be a version of the excitement of an adult world.

The highlights of air-force base mischief were, however, probably those that involved what seemed to us to reflect genuinely military activity. So, oblivious to the danger of what we were doing, we used to slide down the sandbanks of the covered shooting ranges, improvising salients among the piled sandbags that the range contained, and hunting for used cartridges or any other sign of shooting activity. It never occurred to us that a platoon might turn up at any time and start pouring lead into where we were playing. The realisation of another military fantasy was provided at bases at which recently decommissioned aircraft, some of which (even in the mid-1950s) had seen wartime service, were towed to the end of the runway where they were abandoned for several weeks before being destroyed. Among the 'pranged' aircraft were several types of bomber: although the engines had been removed, the craft were otherwise fully functioning, with flaps that flapped, ailerons that went up and down, rudders that swiveled and bomber doors (our way of entry and egress) that opened and shut. There were also wrecks of early British postwar jets such as Vampires and Meteors that were revivified to participate in imaginary dogfights as the indomitable Anson or Brigand light bomber attempted to fend off the fighters' attacks and get through to its destination.

The ultimate pleasure of air-force base life, however, was, after the day's adventures, to repair to the RAF shop or NAAFI and spend pocket money on Mars bars, liquorice and ginger ale before slinking off to some little-frequented corner of the base for a feast at which would also be smoked the cigarettes found in the packs abandoned in derelict air-raid shelters.

DAVID SCOTT is the author of numerous books on art, boxing, poetry, travel, and graphic design. His novel *Dynamo Island: The Cultural History and Geography of a Utopia* was published in 2016, while his translation of Mallarmé's sonnets appeared in 2008. He is Emeritus Professor of French (Textual & Visual Studies) at Trinity College Dublin.

MICHAL AJVAZ, *The Golden Age.*
The Other City.
PIERRE ALBERT-BIROT, *Grabinoulor.*
YUZ ALESHKOVSKY, *Kangaroo.*
SVETLANA ALEXIEVICH, *Voices from Chernobyl.*
FELIPE ALFAU, *Chromos.*
Locos.
JOAO ALMINO, *Enigmas of Spring.*
IVAN ÂNGELO, *The Celebration.*
The Tower of Glass.
ANTÓNIO LOBO ANTUNES, *Knowledge of Hell.*
The Splendor of Portugal.
ALAIN ARIAS-MISSON, *Theatre of Incest.*
JOHN ASHBERY & JAMES SCHUYLER, *A Nest of Ninnies.*
GABRIELA AVIGUR-ROTEM, *Heatwave and Crazy Birds.*
DJUNA BARNES, *Ladies Almanack.*
Ryder.
JOHN BARTH, *Letters.*
Sabbatical.
Collected Stories.
DONALD BARTHELME, *The King.*
Paradise.
SVETISLAV BASARA, *Chinese Letter.*
Fata Morgana.
In Search of the Grail.
MIQUEL BAUÇÀ, *The Siege in the Room.*
RENÉ BELLETTO, *Dying.*
MAREK BIENCZYK, *Transparency.*
ANDREI BITOV, *Pushkin House.*
ANDREJ BLATNIK, *You Do Understand.*
Law of Desire.
LOUIS PAUL BOON, *Chapel Road.*
My Little War.
Summer in Termuren.
ROGER BOYLAN, *Killoyle.*
IGNÁCIO DE LOYOLA BRANDÃO, *Anonymous Celebrity.*
Zero.
BRIGID BROPHY, *In Transit.*
The Prancing Novelist.

GABRIELLE BURTON, *Heartbreak Hotel.*
MICHEL BUTOR, *Degrees.*
Mobile.
G. CABRERA INFANTE, *Infante's Inferno.*
Three Trapped Tigers.
JULIETA CAMPOS, *The Fear of Losing Eurydice.*
ANNE CARSON, *Eros the Bittersweet.*
ORLY CASTEL-BLOOM, *Dolly City.*
LOUIS-FERDINAND CÉLINE, *North.*
Conversations with Professor Y.
London Bridge.
HUGO CHARTERIS, *The Tide Is Right.*
ERIC CHEVILLARD, *Demolishing Nisard.*
The Author and Me.
MARC CHOLODENKO, *Mordechai Schamz.*
EMILY HOLMES COLEMAN, *The Shutter of Snow.*
ERIC CHEVILLARD, *The Author and Me.*
LUIS CHITARRONI, *The No Variations.*
CH'OE YUN, *Mannequin.*
ROBERT COOVER, *A Night at the Movies.*
STANLEY CRAWFORD, *Log of the S.S. The Mrs Unguentine.*
Some Instructions to My Wife.
RALPH CUSACK, *Cadenza.*
NICHOLAS DELBANCO, *Sherbrookes.*
The Count of Concord.
NIGEL DENNIS, *Cards of Identity.*
PETER DIMOCK, *A Short Rhetoric for Leaving the Family.*
ARIEL DORFMAN, *Konfidenz.*
COLEMAN DOWELL, *Island People.*
Too Much Flesh and Jabez.
RIKKI DUCORNET, *Phosphor in Dreamland.*
The Complete Butcher's Tales.
RIKKI DUCORNET (cont.), *The Jade Cabinet.*
The Fountains of Neptune.
WILLIAM EASTLAKE, *Castle Keep.*
Lyric of the Circle Heart.
JEAN ECHENOZ, *Chopin's Move.*

STANLEY ELKIN, *A Bad Man.*
The Dick Gibson Show.
The Franchiser.

FRANÇOIS EMMANUEL, *Invitation to a Voyage.*

SALVADOR ESPRIU, *Ariadne in the Grotesque Labyrinth.*

LESLIE A. FIEDLER, *Love and Death in the American Novel.*

JUAN FILLOY, *Op Oloop.*

GUSTAVE FLAUBERT, *Bouvard and Pécuchet.*

JON FOSSE, *Aliss at the Fire.*
Melancholy.
Trilogy.

FORD MADOX FORD, *The March of Literature.*

MAX FRISCH, *I'm Not Stiller.*
Man in the Holocene.

CARLOS FUENTES, *Christopher Unborn.*
Distant Relations.
Terra Nostra.
Where the Air Is Clear.
Nietzsche on His Balcony.

WILLIAM GADDIS, JR., *The Recognitions.*
JR.

JANICE GALLOWAY, *Foreign Parts.*
The Trick Is to Keep Breathing.

WILLIAM H. GASS, *Life Sentences.*
The Tunnel.
The World Within the Word.
Willie Masters' Lonesome Wife.

GÉRARD GAVARRY, *Hoppla! 1 2 3.*

ETIENNE GILSON, *The Arts of the Beautiful.*
Forms and Substances in the Arts.

C. S. GISCOMBE, *Giscome Road.*
Here.

DOUGLAS GLOVER, *Bad News of the Heart.*

WITOLD GOMBROWICZ, *A Kind of Testament.*

PAULO EMÍLIO SALES GOMES, *P's Three Women.*

GEORGI GOSPODINOV, *Natural Novel.*

JUAN GOYTISOLO, *Juan the Landless.*
Makbara.
Marks of Identity.

JACK GREEN, *Fire the Bastards!*

JIŘÍ GRUŠA, *The Questionnaire.*

MELA HARTWIG, *Am I a Redundant Human Being?*

JOHN HAWKES, *The Passion Artist.*
Whistlejacket.

ELIZABETH HEIGHWAY, ED.,
Contemporary Georgian Fiction.

AIDAN HIGGINS, *Balcony of Europe.*
Blind Man's Bluff.
Bornholm Night-Ferry.
Langrishe, Go Down.
Scenes from a Receding Past.

ALDOUS HUXLEY, *Antic Hay.*
Point Counter Point.
Those Barren Leaves.
Time Must Have a Stop.

JANG JUNG-IL, *When Adam Opens His Eyes*

DRAGO JANČAR, *The Tree with No Name.*
I Saw Her That Night.
Galley Slave.

MIKHEIL JAVAKHISHVILI, *Kvachi.*

GERT JONKE, *The Distant Sound.*
Homage to Czerny.
The System of Vienna.

JACQUES JOUET, *Mountain R.*
Savage.
Upstaged.

JUNG YOUNG-MOON, *A Contrived World.*

MIEKO KANAI, *The Word Book.*

YORAM KANIUK, *Life on Sandpaper.*

ZURAB KARUMIDZE, *Dagny.*

PABLO KATCHADJIAN, *What to Do.*

JOHN KELLY, *From Out of the City.*

HUGH KENNER, *Flaubert, Joyce and Beckett: The Stoic Comedians.*
Joyce's Voices.

DANILO KIŠ, *The Attic.*
The Lute and the Scars.
Psalm 44.
A Tomb for Boris Davidovich.

ANITA KONKKA, *A Fool's Paradise.*

GEORGE KONRÁD, *The City Builder.*
TADEUSZ KONWICKI, *A Minor Apocalypse.*
The Polish Complex.
ELAINE KRAF, *The Princess of 72nd Street.*
JIM KRUSOE, *Iceland.*
AYSE KULIN, *Farewell: A Mansion in Occupied Istanbul.*
EMILIO LASCANO TEGUI, *On Elegance While Sleeping.*
ERIC LAURRENT, *Do Not Touch.*
VIOLETTE LEDUC, *La Bâtarde.*
LEE KI-HO, *At Least We Can Apologize.*
EDOUARD LEVÉ, *Autoportrait.*
Suicide.
MARIO LEVI, *Istanbul Was a Fairy Tale.*
DEBORAH LEVY, *Billy and Girl.*
JOSÉ LEZAMA LIMA, *Paradiso.*
OSMAN LINS, *Avalovara.*
The Queen of the Prisons of Greece.
ALF MACLOCHLAINN, *Out of Focus.*
Past Habitual.
RON LOEWINSOHN, *Magnetic Field(s).*
YURI LOTMAN, *Non-Memoirs.*
D. KEITH MANO, *Take Five.*
MINA LOY, *Stories and Essays of Mina Loy.*
MICHELINE AHARONIAN MARCOM, *The Mirror in the Well.*
BEN MARCUS, *The Age of Wire and String.*
WALLACE MARKFIELD, *Teitlebaum's Window.*
To an Early Grave.
DAVID MARKSON, *Reader's Block.*
Wittgenstein's Mistress.
CAROLE MASO, *AVA.*
HISAKI MATSUURA, *Triangle.*
LADISLAV MATEJKA & KRYSTYNA POMORSKA, EDS., *Readings in Russian Poetics: Formalist & Structuralist Views.*
HARRY MATHEWS, *Cigarettes.*
The Conversions.
The Human Country.
The Journalist.
My Life in CIA.

Singular Pleasures.
The Sinking of the Odradek.
Stadium.
Tlooth.
JOSEPH MCELROY, *Night Soul and Other Stories.*
ABDELWAHAB MEDDEB, *Talismano.*
GERHARD MEIER, *Isle of the Dead.*
HERMAN MELVILLE, *The Confidence-Man.*
AMANDA MICHALOPOULOU, *I'd Like.*
STEVEN MILLHAUSER, *The Barnum Museum.*
In the Penny Arcade.
RALPH J. MILLS, JR., *Essays on Poetry.*
CHRISTINE MONTALBETTI, *The Origin of Man.*
Western.
NICHOLAS MOSLEY, *Accident.*
Assassins.
Catastrophe Practice.
Hopeful Monsters.
Imago Bird.
Natalie Natalia.
Serpent.
WARREN MOTTE, *Fiction Now: The French Novel in the 21st Century.*
Oulipo: A Primer of Potential Literature.
GERALD MURNANE, *Barley Patch.*
Inland.
YVES NAVARRE, *Our Share of Time.*
Sweet Tooth.
DOROTHY NELSON, *In Night's City.*
Tar and Feathers.
WILFRIDO D. NOLLEDO, *But for the Lovers.*
BORIS A. NOVAK, *The Master of Insomnia.*
FLANN O'BRIEN, *At Swim-Two-Birds.*
The Best of Myles.
The Dalkey Archive.
The Hard Life.
The Poor Mouth.
The Third Policeman.
CLAUDE OLLIER, *The Mise-en-Scène.*
Wert and the Life Without End.

PATRIK OUŘEDNÍK, *Europeana.*
The Opportune Moment, 1855.

BORIS PAHOR, *Necropolis.*

FERNANDO DEL PASO, *News from the Empire.*
Palinuro of Mexico.

ROBERT PINGET, *The Inquisitory.*
Mahu or The Material.
Trio.

MANUEL PUIG, *Betrayed by Rita Hayworth.*
The Buenos Aires Affair.
Heartbreak Tango.

RAYMOND QUENEAU, *The Last Days.*
Odile.
Pierrot Mon Ami.
Saint Glinglin.

ANN QUIN, *Berg.*
Passages.
Three.
Tripticks.

ISHMAEL REED, *The Free-Lance Pallbearers.*
The Last Days of Louisiana Red.
Ishmael Reed: The Plays.
Juice!
The Terrible Threes.
The Terrible Twos.
Yellow Back Radio Broke-Down.

RAINER MARIA RILKE,
The Notebooks of Malte Laurids Brigge.

JULIÁN RÍOS, *The House of Ulysses.*
Larva: A Midsummer Night's Babel.
Poundemonium.

ALAIN ROBBE-GRILLET, *Project for a Revolution in New York.*
A Sentimental Novel.

AUGUSTO ROA BASTOS, *I the Supreme.*

DANIËL ROBBERECHTS, *Arriving in Avignon.*

JEAN ROLIN, *The Explosion of the Radiator Hose.*

OLIVIER ROLIN, *Hotel Crystal.*

ALIX CLEO ROUBAUD, *Alix's Journal.*

JACQUES ROUBAUD, *The Form of a City Changes Faster, Alas, Than the Human Heart.*

The Great Fire of London.
Hortense in Exile.
Hortense Is Abducted.
Mathematics: The Plurality of Worlds of Lewis.
Some Thing Black.

RAYMOND ROUSSEL, *Impressions of Africa.*

VEDRANA RUDAN, *Night.*

GERMAN SADULAEV, *The Maya Pill.*

TOMAŽ ŠALAMUN, *Soy Realidad.*

LYDIE SALVAYRE, *The Company of Ghosts.*

LUIS RAFAEL SÁNCHEZ, *Macho Camacho's Beat.*

SEVERO SARDUY, *Cobra & Maitreya.*

NATHALIE SARRAUTE, *Do You Hear Them?*
Martereau.
The Planetarium.

STIG SÆTERBAKKEN, *Siamese.*
Self-Control.
Through the Night.

ARNO SCHMIDT, *Collected Novellas.*
Collected Stories.
Nobodaddy's Children.
Two Novels.

ASAF SCHURR, *Motti.*

GAIL SCOTT, *My Paris.*

JUNE AKERS SEESE,
Is This What Other Women Feel Too?

BERNARD SHARE, *Inish.*
Transit.

VIKTOR SHKLOVSKY, *Bowstring.*
Literature and Cinematography.
Theory of Prose.
Third Factory.
Zoo, or Letters Not about Love.

PIERRE SINIAC, *The Collaborators.*

KJERSTI A. SKOMSVOLD,
The Faster I Walk, the Smaller I Am.

JOSEF ŠKVORECKÝ, *The Engineer of Human Souls.*

GILBERT SORRENTINO, *Aberration of Starlight.*
Blue Pastoral.
Crystal Vision.

Imaginative Qualities of Actual Things.
Mulligan Stew.
Red the Fiend.
Steelwork.
Under the Shadow.
ANDRZEJ STASIUK, *Dukla.*
Fado.
GERTRUDE STEIN, *The Making of Americans.*
A Novel of Thank You.
PIOTR SZEWC, *Annihilation.*
GONÇALO M. TAVARES, *A Man: Klaus Klump.*
Jerusalem.
Learning to Pray in the Age of Technique.
LUCIAN DAN TEODOROVICI, *Our Circus Presents...*
NIKANOR TERATOLOGEN, *Assisted Living.*
STEFAN THEMERSON, *Hobson's Island.*
The Mystery of the Sardine.
Tom Harris.
JOHN TOOMEY, *Sleepwalker.*
Huddleston Road.
Slipping.
DUMITRU TSEPENEAG, *Hotel Europa.*
The Necessary Marriage.
Pigeon Post.
Vain Art of the Fugue.
La Belle Roumaine.
Waiting: Stories.
ESTHER TUSQUETS, *Stranded.*
DUBRAVKA UGRESIC, *Lend Me Your Character.*
Thank You for Not Reading.
TOR ULVEN, *Replacement.*
MATI UNT, *Brecht at Night.*
Diary of a Blood Donor.
Things in the Night.
ÁLVARO URIBE & OLIVIA SEARS, EDS., *Best of Contemporary Mexican Fiction.*
ELOY URROZ, *Friction.*
The Obstacles.
LUISA VALENZUELA, *Dark Desires and the Others.*
He Who Searches.

PAUL VERHAEGHEN, *Omega Minor.*
BORIS VIAN, *Heartsnatcher.*
TOOMAS VINT, *An Unending Landscape.*
ORNELA VORPSI, *The Country Where No One Ever Dies.*
AUSTRYN WAINHOUSE, *Hedyphagetica.*
MARKUS WERNER, *Cold Shoulder.*
Zundel's Exit.
CURTIS WHITE, *The Idea of Home.*
Memories of My Father Watching TV.
Requiem.
DIANE WILLIAMS, *Excitability: Selected Stories.*
DOUGLAS WOOLF, *Wall to Wall.*
Ya! & John-Juan.
JAY WRIGHT, *Polynomials and Pollen.*
The Presentable Art of Reading Absence.
PHILIP WYLIE, *Generation of Vipers.*
MARGUERITE YOUNG, *Angel in the Forest.*
Miss MacIntosh, My Darling.
REYOUNG, *Unbabbling.*
ZORAN ŽIVKOVIĆ, *Hidden Camera.*
LOUIS ZUKOFSKY, *Collected Fiction.*
VITOMIL ZUPAN, *Minuet for Guitar.*
SCOTT ZWIREN, *God Head.*

AND MORE...